SEVEN DAYS

SEVEN DAYS

REBEKA SHAID

WALKER
BOOKS

In loving memory of Peter David Reynolds (1984–2016).
We carry your heart.

First published 2024 by Walker Books Ltd
87 Vauxhall Walk, London SE11 5HJ

2 4 6 8 10 9 7 5 3

Text © 2024 Rebeka Shaid
Cover and interior illustrations © 2024 Parvati Pillai

The right of Rebeka Shaid to be identified as author of this
work has been asserted in accordance with the
Copyright, Designs and Patents Act 1988

This book has been typeset in Bembo Book

Printed and bound by CPI Group (UK) Ltd, Croydon CR0 4YY

British Library Cataloguing in Publication Data:
a catalogue record for this book is available from the British Library

ISBN 978-1-5295-1396-7

www.walker.co.uk

MIX
Paper | Supporting
responsible forestry
FSC
www.fsc.org
FSC® C171272

where are you from i asked
he smiled in mockery and said
one half from the east
one half from the west
one half made of water and earth
one half made of heart and soul
one half staying at the shores and
one half nesting in a pearl

Rumi

DAY 1

1
noori

Urgent meeting requested. Now!

Noori hit the send button and waited for a reply from Mai – her mate, one-time babysitter and next-door neighbour. It arrived within seconds.

What happened? Mai's response read.

My dad's got a horrible secret. Can't keep it to myself any more.

Nah, don't be stupid. Your dad's lovely, so chubby and nice.

Don't be gross.

As she strutted on, Noori glanced up from her cracked phone screen. She'd wandered off the dirt path, taking a shortcut through the park, and she found herself now staring at a ruddy-faced male jogger in his forties who was gasping for air. He reminded Noori of her father. Maybe it was the doughy belly, the marshmallow nose or the drops of sweat on his balding head. That was what her dad must look like when he did his daily circuit runs around the Downs.

The breathless jogger squinted at Noori, embarrassment flicking in his eyes. He lacked stamina, but at least this guy was trying. The same couldn't be said about her father.

Before Noori was able to finish that thought, her mobile started to vibrate, the rhythmic drumbeats of a familiar ringtone spicing up the air of this provincial English city that used to feel like home. Not any more.

Noori swiped her thumb across the screen, sighing into the phone.

"What's going on?" Mai asked suspiciously. "You got into another fight with your dad?"

"Yes. He's *so* ... ugh."

"Is it about Pakistan?" Mai probed.

"It's not like I'm dropping out of school; I'm *switching* schools. Besides, I know lots of people who've gone on a year abroad," Noori said, unable to think of a single person who had done what she was planning on doing.

Noori's temporary move to Pakistan was more than a study-abroad thing. It was a pilgrimage. Sort of.

"I know you need to let off some steam, but I have to finish packing," Mai said. "Can we postpone our urgent meeting by an hour or so?"

"Nope," Noori said firmly. "Urgent means urgent. Meet me you know where."

"Uh…"

"At our bench!"

"Fine." Pause. "I'll come now."

Noori hung up and slowed her step. No need to rush. It

would take Mai a few minutes to get to their meeting point. The bench. It wasn't really Mai and Noori's bench. It used to be Munazzah and Noori's bench. But Munazzah was a goner. And Noori missed her. Munazzah was her best bud and cousin, who had died eight months ago in a small Punjabi village thousands of miles away, in what can only be described as a freak incident.

Death's a bastard, Noori thought. The worst kind of butthole out there. It made no sense how Munazzah had been alive one moment and was gone the next. Everyone was born with an expiry date, but Munazzah's had come too soon.

Could it have been prevented? Noori asked herself this question over and over. Or was it bad luck, as her dad had claimed, pulling Noori in for a hug and letting her sob on his shoulder until his shirt was soaked with tears and snot. They had cried together then, feeling each other's pain, their bruised hearts beating to the same sad beat. But that was months ago. And Dad wasn't the same Dad, just like Noori wasn't the same Noori.

Too much had happened and too many hostile words had been spoken. Noori was the only one who knew about Dad's secret. She had a right to be furious.

Her father was annoyed for a different reason. "You can't just quit," he'd told her, making it sound like she was abandoning him rather than simply going to experience the world. Well, in seven days Noori would be out of here, leaving Bristol behind, leaving her family behind, leaving it all behind. For twelve months.

Noori wiped a salty tear from her chin, a streak of sadness marking her acne-prone skin. She hated crying, and angry crying was worse than ordinary crying. Why was she always filled with fury? Shouldn't mourning a family member feel depressing, brain-numbing, heart-dying?

Noori wasn't depressed. Her brain was active, flipping into radical Noori mode. And her heart was beating strong and steady. There was nothing wrong with her. She was fine and dandy, alive and breathing – but.

"But what?" she roared at a puffy cloud that had the impertinence to look beautiful and at peace in the bright blue sky.

Noori strained her neck, glaring at the horizon until she felt the sun burning away at her corneas. She could handle that kind of pain. It was sharp and vicious, but it passed. Her eyesight might not recover, but her soul would. And what did Munazzah's favourite Sufi poet Rumi say? "Nothing can nourish the soul but light." Noori had followed Rumi's advice, but it turned out the light of the sun wasn't powerful enough to heal her wounded spirit.

With a soul as heavy as a fat hippo, she carried on towards the bench. It used to be the nicest spot in her whole small world. Munazzah and Noori would hang out there together. Her cousin had been almost two years older than Noori and a million soul years ahead of her. "You're the wise one in the family," Noori would hear her mum whisper, giving her niece a loving look usually reserved for her own children.

The Oates household consisted of Noori, her parents and her twin siblings, plus Munazzah. She had been one of them, an indispensable part of their tribe. Of course, Munazzah had had her own family, made up of her parents and a plump beagle called Doughnut (because he looked like one curled up in his scruffy nest). But Munazzah had been an only child and had lived round the corner from Noori, here in hilly Bristol.

They had grown up together. She had been Noori's first friend and best friend. And now Noori had lost her.

There had been notable differences between the two of them.

Munazzah was small and lanky; Noori was stocky and tall.

Munazzah was a pacifist; Noori loved to battle.

Munazzah was a saint; Noori was a rebel.

Noori, who considered herself a warrior and a playwright in the making, never obeyed and always picked a fight. How often had she complained to Munazzah about her overprotective parents? Her cousin would nod along, never interrupting, always waiting until Noori's tirade had finished. And, eventually, lovely Munazzah would gaze Noori in the eye and say: "Sounds like you're PMSing, sis."

And she would be right, like she always was.

Noori rubbed her snotty nose, wondering why life felt so cold although it was August and the sun was warming her skin, shining on her henna hair.

She had no idea how to handle the matter with her dad, but Mai would – even though she wasn't Munazzah. Where her cousin had quoted Rumi, Noori's next-door neighbour Instagrammed arty pictures of French cheese. Still, Mai was an elder – by two years to be precise – attending the same class as

Munazzah. And thanks to Mai, Noori now nailed the perfect winged eyeliner and donned the sandal and mismatched socks look with confidence.

Mai wasn't Munazzah, but she was one of the few people Noori could count on. Always.

Noori picked up her speed, her sandals bouncing on the soft grass, her breath quickening. And there was Mai, sitting on their bench, wearing an unflattering hoody. The time had come to speak the truth.

2
aamir

This moment, if viewed from a skewed angle, was epic. Sure, a bunch of criminals had mugged him a few hours ago, snatched his money and phone, but … he was free. And freedom, paired with solitude, was epic.

Aamir stretched his legs, letting his weight sink into the bench. This park was nice. He had fond childhood memories of the place, had come here numerous times with his family whenever they had visited the zoo. It was bittersweet to be back, to remember a world that had once been whole. He and his older brother Bilal used to fly their kites up here while their parents watched their sons with pride.

A gentle breeze rolled over the cliffs. The grass swayed from left to right, dancing to a slow tune. The sun sparkled and glistened, the air was clear, sweetened by the summer breeze that heightened his senses, and a soothing stillness surrounded him. Aamir was filled with faint hope.

Being skint and a loser felt all right here, on a random bench in this not-so-random city. Aamir owned nothing now, other than his backpack that contained some of his clothes, a bottle of water, a book and a pack of unsalted peanuts he had chucked in on a whim, plus a bag of toiletries and a framed photograph of Maa.

In a way, owning next to nothing and being reduced to this anonymous state of nobodiness was liberating. He didn't have to pretend to be anybody, and who was Aamir Inayat Mahmood anyway?

He had slipped into different roles all his life. At home, in school, playing rugby, at the mosque, and with Claire. He could never please that girl. There was always something wrong with him. She wanted him to wear certain clothes, speak in a certain way, act in a certain manner, until she turned him into the fakest version of himself. Aamir wasn't good enough for Claire, and yet she professed to love him. Argh. *How* did she still get under his skin?

"Good riddance," Aamir muttered to himself, adjusting his hoody and tucking his arms underneath it.

He shivered. It almost felt like he was coming down with something, but then he'd felt off since coming down with "the rona" a few weeks ago. Like his chest always felt tight and he'd find himself short of breath at random times of the day. Or night.

Plus, the thugs who had attacked him at the train station had given him a proper beating. His head was thumping and no matter how hard he rubbed his eyes, he seemed to be looking through a smudged lens. Or maybe he was just dehydrated. He hadn't eaten or drunk anything since sneaking out of his father's Cardiff flat early that morning.

Aamir rummaged around the backpack until he found a squashed plastic bottle and took a sip of water. He needed to find a place to refill it soon. Maybe that library he had passed on his way up the hill. And then? What would Bilal say if Aamir showed up out of the blue, looking for a place to crash so he could lie low, sort his life out, and come to terms with what had happened back home?

Would Bilal understand? Probably not. The two brothers used to be close, despite the eight-year age gap. Bilal was a proper big brother, his only sibling, someone who knew what it was like to grow up under their father's religious regime. But then he'd decided to get hitched, giving in to parental expectations by having an arranged marriage, wedding a good girl from a good family.

Aamir never thought Bilal would be interested in hooking up with someone he met through their matchmaking mother. They used to take the piss out of an older cousin for marrying a woman he'd met twice before putting a ring on her finger. It came as something of a shocker when Bilal announced his intention to stick with Mahmood marital traditions.

Their big brother/little brother relationship had changed now that Bilal was someone's husband. Life had gone downhill ever since. It was as if Aamir hadn't only lost *her*; he had also lost his brother. Truth was, their family was broken. Aamir was broken – like an old record that had long forgotten how to play its tune.

Reality dawned on Aamir then. What the hell had he been thinking? There was nothing epic about his newly gained sense of freedom and solitude. This city had him trapped.

Yeah, he could amble down to the harbourside, where Bilal and his pregnant wife lived in a fancy flat with views of the water. He could ring the bell and wait for his kind sister-in-law to answer the door, confused to find him there. But then he'd have a whole lot of explaining to do when Bilal returned home from work and started interrogating Aamir, blaming him for causing their father additional heartache.

He could picture the scene vividly. The two brothers, standing eye to eye, both wondering how things could have gone so wrong. Bilal would stare him down, questioning Aamir. "What are you doing here? What have you done this time? Why aren't you home with Abbu?" It wouldn't even cross his mind that maybe it was Pa who had kicked Aamir out, leaving his younger son to make his own way in the world without having a clue what to do and where to go.

All Aamir could hope for was that sometime in the future he would look back, remember this weird sitting-on-a-bench-in-Bristol moment and have a bloody good laugh. None of this would matter then. All his worries would be gone and he'd be OK…

He felt a dull pain in his chest and instinctively placed a palm on his heart. There was a longing, a thirst.

After pouring the last drop of water down his throat, Aamir stuffed the bottle back into the rucksack, his eyes glimpsing the book as he did so. A weak smile spread across his face. That slim paperback of poetry had found its way into his bag. He hadn't given it much thought this morning when he had packed in a rushed, semi-drunken state and caught the first train to Bristol.

Aamir tried to sigh out his worries, without success. He pinched the book, folding it open on his lap to stare at a random line. He wasn't a man of faith, but he believed in the randomness of the universe.

"Where are you from?" the book was asking.

Aamir pondered. Where *was* he from? He dived deep into the question, taking only the faintest notice of the slow footsteps creeping up behind him, moving closer until coming to a complete halt.

A person, a girl wearing black sandals and mismatched unicorn socks, plopped down next to him on the bench, exclaiming five angry words.

"Man, I hate my dad."

3
noori

"He's a liar," Noori said, ranting like an angry camel. "He's a wolf dressed in sheepskin, or shepherd skin, or whatever. Actually, wolves are innocent and can't help themselves. They'll die if they don't eat sheep, so Dad is more like a tarantula that sheds skin whenever—"

Oops.

Noori's eyes grew wide and her cheeks turned hot, sizzling like a warm dollop of ghee on spicy daal. The person sharing the bench with her wasn't Mai; it was a desi dude. Black hair, big under-eye circles, brown skin but slightly different breed. He was of the creamy chocolate fudge variant; she was a tough butter toffee gal. He couldn't be much older than her, a scruffy uni student maybe.

She scanned his exterior, her trained eyes skimming over his battered pair of trainers (Converse, nice), taking in the cracked skin on his hands (typical case of boy neglecting skincare) and the dark bruise on one of his smooth cheek-bones (ouch).

He was gripping a slim book. It looked like a collection of poems, judging by the gaps between each paragraph. He was probably reading philosophy or English lit – he had to be a softie just acting like a toughie in stained pipe jeans with broad, sloped shoulders and hairy knuckles. At night, she mused, he'd write love letters to his beloved and sob in secret over dead ducklings or run-over squirrels.

Noori patted herself on the back. She had sussed this number out without even speaking to him – but hold on. Was the guy reading Rumi, as in Munazzah's...? Noori's heart stopped beating. A flash of lightning struck her soul. Was this the sign she'd been waiting for? Because Noori believed in signs – big time.

When she'd received Munazzah's postcard *six months after* her cousin had died – like everything else, the postal service couldn't be trusted – Noori's eyes fell on that last line written in Munazzah's messy yet bubbly handwriting. "You should come to Pakistan, moron." *Moron* had been a term of endearment between the cousins. And it was the sign Noori needed to follow Munazzah's final call and take her size eight feet to the motherland, which (according to Google) was exactly five thousand two hundred and eighty-four miles away from where Noori was currently standing and staring at this book.

Not just any book, but the Rumi book that the scruffy chocolate fudge guy was gripping in his hand. It was another sign, a moment of synchronicity. Munazzah had owned that very book and it now dozed in Noori's bedroom, perched on a dusty bookshelf, longing to be read, and understood, and heard.

She glanced at the boy again, reassessing his entire existence in a stunned second of silence. He twisted his head sideways to face her, his straight nose opposing hers, a frown wrinkling his forehead. They gawked at each other as he removed his hoody, revealing a messy bun of black hair.

What *was* that smell? He must have showered in cologne, spraying a potent combo of musk and zesty fruit all over him. Noori took another sniff, detecting a subtle hint of magnolia and pink pepper — she liked to think she had a well-honed sense of smell. In reality, who knew? But whatever it was, it smelled nice. His eyes seemed familiar; they were big and muddy, all malty and gritty.

Noori felt a need to speak, which wasn't unusual since she always felt a need to speak.

"You reading Rumi?" she asked, pointing her sharp middle finger at the book.

"Sometimes."

"*Très* cool."

Jeez, she never mixed French and English — didn't even know French apart from the odd food-related word. Macron was her favourite, or was it macaron?

The dude — Punjabi, Bengali, who knew? — inched away from Noori, shuffling down the bench. He seemed a little unnerved by her presence; he probably thought she was a bit off, bad-mouthing her dad in front of a stranger. Noori felt the familiar need to explain herself.

"Thought you were someone else," she said. "Not wearing my glasses today and you looked like my friend. I mean, I thought you did. Never mind."

"OK."

"So. Where are you from?" Noori asked, and he gave her the weirdest stare in the world, as though she had spoken to his soul or quoted a heart-opening Rumi line.

He was ogling her in a non-pervy way. Had she said something inappropriate? Her parents obviously advised her against speaking to strangers; enquiring about their geographical origin was also a no-go. But then, Noori always did the opposite of what they expected her to do. It was her way of letting them know she was an independent sixteen-year-old.

"Haven't seen you around before," she observed. "You at uni here?"

He shook his head. "No."

"Funny."

"What?"

"Nothing. I mean…" Noori stroked the bushy eyebrows that Mai longed to pluck, but every time her friend approached with a pair of tweezers, she slapped them away. "I just thought. You kind of struck me as an English student, that's all."

"An English student?"

"Yeah, lounging in the park on a sunny Friday, reading poetry, that's what they tend to get up to. My dad's a history prof and I see his students all the time; the city is full of them, you know?"

He nodded in bemusement.

She ploughed on. "So you're from Brizzle?" she asked.

"Huh?"

"Bris*tol*," Noori said slowly, slipping out of her regional accent. "You're not a local then."

"No." He shrugged his shoulders.

Noori knew that type of shrug: it was a Punjabi shrug; she was sure of it. Having binged on millions of Bollywood films and taken part in many Bhangra dance classes, she could spot a Punjabi shrug from miles away. This desi dude wasn't an ordinary desi dude; he was a Punjabi desi dude.

But was he a Pakistani Punjabi or an Indian Punjabi? Noori's maternal grandparents didn't distinguish between the two. They were born before Pakistan was born, years before India was split apart. Stupid colonialists. Noori blamed colonialism and its afterlife for many evils. Brexit, to name one.

"So why do you hate your dad?" the boy asked, finding his voice again.

"What do you mean?"

"You called him a wolf."

Noori sighed. "I don't really *hate* him; I just don't like him right now."

"He loathes your boyfriend or, uh, girlfriend?"

Noori blushed. "Nah."

"What's he done?"

"It's unforgivable, that's all I'll say."

"Sounds bad."

"It is. He should be ashamed of himself."

The boy nodded again. "Yeah, this thing about shame; it plays a role in our culture," he said.

"*Our* culture?"

He shrugged again, and Noori couldn't resist the urge to ask him another question. Most people didn't spark her interest, because most people were boring. But for some peculiar reason she wanted to know more about this boy, like *who* he was.

"So what's your name?" she asked.

"Aamir."

Noori nodded. A suitable name, she thought.

"I'm Mahnoor," she said. "But everyone calls me Noori."

4
aamir

Mahnoor sounded way nicer than Noori.

It was a name Aamir had come across before. He had watched a film once, one of those melodramatic black and white ones that his maa used to love. And during the closing credits, right after everyone had been killed, Aamir had spotted that name. Mahnoor. It had stood out. Even after all these years he still remembered that movie, and that name, and what his mother had murmured to him afterwards.

"Jaisi karni waisi bharni, beta," Maa had said. *As you sow, so shall you reap, son.*

His seeds must have been foul. There was nothing to reap. And his land, his earth, was soiled, stained with memories, flooded by polluted water.

"Tell me," Mahnoor said, "what kind of desi are you?"

He stared at her. "What does that even mean?"

"I bet you're Pakistani."

"I'm British."

"Yeah, yeah. But I'm talking about your roots."

"I'm not a tree."

"But if you were, you'd be a mango tree and not an English oak?"

She smiled. He didn't. Why was she interrogating him? They were both strangers to each other and Aamir wasn't used to people enquiring about his ethnic origin. This *baji* was different. She looked like the girls in his community – henna hair, gold bangles, cat eyes – but she didn't really resemble any of them. She was direct, blunt and didn't seem to care what anyone thought of her. One glimpse at her unicorn socks said it all.

"Do you speak Urdu?" Mahnoor asked, still cross-examining him.

"Not really."

"Oh. That's a shame"

There was that word again. Aamir hated the implications it carried. According to his father, he had brought shame to his family. Aamir hadn't broken any rules – in fact he'd managed to live his life without harming anyone whatsoever – but Pa still took offence. It wasn't proper to do this, or to do that. There was only one way, and it was his father's way. The truth was, it had all gone apeshit eight months ago when Maa had exited this life.

He missed her.

So much, it was killing him inside.

But so it goes.

"What's that stink?" Mahnoor asked, wrinkling her freckled nose.

Aamir blinked. He was aware of his body odour, but he didn't think it was that bad. Self-conscious, he edged away from her. The last time he had showered was over twenty hours ago. He'd left home unwashed, unkempt, and unfit to make such a life-changing decision as running away, a choice that would determine the rest of his uncertain future.

"People are smoking weed somewhere; I can smell it," Mahnoor said, nose in the air like a sniffer dog. "I was born with a sensitive snout."

"I can't smell anything," Aamir mumbled, shifting in his seat under her hard gaze.

"Really? It's contaminating the air. So gross."

"It's not that gross."

"You smoke weed?" Mahnoor gave him another hard gaze.

"I didn't say that. Forget what I said."

His cheeks were blazing. Aamir should have anticipated that reaction. Mahnoor might come across as unusual, but she was still judgemental, like most people in his community.

"I'd totally smoke some if it wasn't for the smell. So disgusting," she said.

Or not. This girl was a samosa: full of surprises. For one crazy moment he believed this whole thing wasn't a coincidence. Maybe he was meant to meet her today, on that bench.

What a load of bollocks.

Life was nothing but a series of random incidents, some good, some terrible. Aamir knew that all too well. If there was one thing he had learned in the seventeen years he had dwelt on this planet, it was that ups and downs were part of the deal. And what a crappy deal he'd been handed.

"By the way," Mahnoor said, tapping her temple. "You're bleeding."

5
noori

"Hey, are you about to faint?" Noori asked. "It's not that serious, just a small laceration."

"I can't see blood, makes me—" Aamir shut his eyes, his head tilting to the side.

"Woozy? I can tell."

Aamir didn't respond. His upper body shifted into a Tower of Pisa position, one shoulder leaning forward. Noori felt a tad sorry for him. His skin colour had turned from mocha to latte, not a happy sign. And she couldn't offer anything to make him feel better. After arguing with her dad this morning, Noori had stomped out of the house in a hurry, forgetting to grab her handbag. She wanted to run to the ice cream van to fetch Aamir a lolly but she didn't have any cash on her. The only thing she could give him was cinnamon-flavoured gum. She tugged it out of her jeans pocket, handing it to him.

"Here, chew this."

"What. Is. It."

"Man. Open your eyes and take a look."

"Can't. Sick."

Noori unwrapped the gum with skilled precision. She was used to handling patients. Her twin siblings were younger than her and she couldn't remember the number of times she had to deal with their ouchies, both big and small.

"Open your mouth," she ordered.

To her surprise, Aamir complied and Noori found herself analysing his immaculate row of gnashers. Damn it! Why did she even notice these things? She shoved the strip into his mouth and took pleasure from watching him chew on the gum that would release its sweet flavour in no time.

She tended to his wound next. There wasn't a lot of blood, just a trickle running down his temple. If she hadn't mentioned it, he would never have known. Noori produced a tissue from her bra – she liked to keep them in a warm place – and applied pressure to the cut. It was hardly bleeding now.

"You'll be fine," Noori said. "This minor ailment should not affect your life expectancy."

"Thanks," Aamir murmured, still pressing his lids together.

"So what happened: did you knock your head or something?"

"A bunch of idiots knocked my head."

"I hate idiots." Noori sniffed for no reason. "Did you punch back?"

"Of course."

"Good. The only way to beat a bully is to beat a bully, 's what I say."

Aamir flipped his eyes open, giving Noori another weird stare. Rumi knows what he was thinking, not that Noori usually cared. She wasn't interested in other people's opinions. It was her opinion that counted, end of story. But why, dear Rumi, did she wonder what thoughts were swirling around in Aamir's brain?

There was something about his eyes. They were freaky. It was like gazing into a brimming cup of tea, except the tea changed shades, turning into Darjeeling, and then Ceylon, and every now and again someone chucked a handful of spices into the mug. Turmeric. Cardamom. Ginger. Something was brewing. Maybe it was time to take the teabag out and see what this mysterious potion was made of. Maybe… Oh, get a grip, woman!

"Feeling better?" Noori asked, folding the blood-flecked tissue into a neat rectangle and handing it back to him. For a split second she thought about keeping it. ARGH.

"Yeah." Aamir placed a hand on his stomach, as if to calm his nerves. He still looked latte. "Thanks for the gum."

"Don't mention it."

He swallowed. "I don't know why it happens. The blood thing."

"An evolutionary gift, a caveman instinct or something," Noori said. "When you get into a fight and spot blood, you faint. Makes your opponent think you're dead, hence increasing your chances of survival."

"That makes it sound all right. Should have told that to my rugby mates."

"You play rugby?"

"Used to. I prefer cricket."

"Me too. I watch it with my dad, but we don't support the same team." Noori pursed her lips.

She was mulling over her dad dilemma again. There was a time, not that long ago, when Noori had appreciated her father for who he was. Despite being a lecturer in medieval history – why, just *why*? – he was smart. He could even be witty if he tried hard enough. She had believed he was a good guy who had always taken a genuine interest in his children, in *her*. Showing the twins how to play the piano (Noori refused; it wasn't her jam), or taking Noori to the Bhangra class she used to attend with Munazzah.

It was Dad who had convinced her to keep going after Munazzah's death, even when she didn't want to. Not without her cousin. But Dad insisted; he would drive her to classes, and he even joined in despite seriously lacking any rhythmical skill and flexibility. It was actually a little worrying to watch at times. Yet, when Noori had attempted to teach her father the single *dhamaal*, a move that required coordinated hopping and bouncing and plenty of shoulder shaking, her dad had given his best. He had made the effort. He had shown Noori he cared.

Now Noori was wiser.

If only Munazzah were here to give her a much-needed piece of advice, and a hug. She half expected to hear her cousin's soft-spoken voice then, but someone else was speaking to her.

"Noori?" Mai asked, somewhat baffled.

Her bud had arrived late, as always. Mai looked amazing, as if ready to go on holiday right this minute even though her annual family trip to the South of France was still two days away. She was wearing a stripy top and had tied a chiffon scarf around her neck, her jet-black hair tumbling down to her waist.

Mai's eyes wandered to Aamir, who looked dazed and not with it. She raised a brow, wagging her head as if sending a secret message to her friend that Noori failed to decode.

"Good to see you," Noori said, addressing Mai. "You got any money?"

"Um…"

"Can you buy me an ice lolly, please? The van's parked over there, look."

The ice cream van was in plain sight, a merry family group queuing up for their treats. They'd probably head to the zoo in a bit or have a picnic and play Frisbee.

"You want ice cream. For real?" Mai asked, her small eyes still fixed on Aamir.

"Not an ice cream, a lolly, please. One of those fruit lollies, you know the ones, right?" Noori asked.

Mai nodded, sighing.

Noori beamed at her friend, who parted her blushed lips but said nothing, her confused gaze flitting between Noori and Aamir. After a moment of non-verbal communication — Mai kept twitching her eyebrows and Noori had no idea what that meant — Mai took reluctant steps towards the ice cream van, throwing Noori a cryptic glance over her shoulder.

"That's the friend I told you about," Noori said, nodding at Aamir. "The one I thought was you, sitting on the bench."

"I've never been confused for a Chinese girl before."

"She's not Chinese. Her mum's a Frenchwoman from Vietnam."

Aamir scratched his head. "And you thought I was her?"

"I told you: I'm not wearing my glasses."

"I see."

A slow smile crept over Aamir's face. He looked so different when he smiled, and Noori couldn't help but goggle at his teeth again. They were a beautiful white, not bleachy at all, but the crisp white of a peeled sugar cane. Noori adored sugar canes. A few years ago, one of her mum's aunties in Pakistan had sent over a plastic bag filled with sugar canes. Noori and Munazzah had spent hours sucking and chewing the juicy liquid out of those scrumptious sticks.

"Catch," Mai said, materializing out of nowhere.

She dropped the ice lolly into Noori's lap, still twitching her brows. Noori ignored her friend's pointed body language and handed Aamir the lolly.

"After your fainting spell, I think you need this more than me," Noori said. Aamir hesitated, making no move to accept it. "Just take it. It'll help with the dizziness."

When he eventually took the lolly, he looked so grateful, although he tried to hide it. Aamir seemed to be the kind of guy who kept quiet and concealed stuff.

Noori wondered why.

6
aamir

It was a gift from the heavens, the most delicious food Aamir had ever savoured, except for Maa's daal, and silky spinach, and fluffy rotis, and … never mind. This was what his body needed right now, a cooling lick of ice lolly, the synthetic fruit flavours dissolving blissfully on his watery tongue.

"Can I speak to you for a mo?" the friend asked Mahnoor in a tight voice.

"Sure. What's up?"

"In private."

It was obvious that Mai didn't like him. She viewed Aamir with suspicion, he could tell. She had given him a horrified look when she first laid eyes on him, as though he was a thug, and Aamir was anything but. He might not have been the good boy Pa hoped he'd become, but he was a good enough person. Sort of.

Maa had thought of him as a good boy. Whenever Aamir

had helped out in the kitchen, chopping vegetables or kneading soft roti dough, she'd pat his hand and plant a breezy kiss on top of his head. "You're my heart and my world," she used to say, in her language. She took pride in both her boys, but they all knew Aamir was a mummy's boy.

His brother was different. Bilal was more single-minded, going after his goals, sticking to rules and rational thinking, never discussing emotions – much like their father. They had failed Maa, Aamir realized in an unpleasant moment of clarity. Pa, Bilal, Aamir – they were not the family Maa would have wanted them to be.

Maa would have been horrified to know Aamir had run away from home after insulting his father and his heritage, and was now drifting around Bristol, hanging out at a bench like a homeless person when he still had a family that cared. Or so he hoped. Taking off with nothing but a backpack had seemed like a good idea this morning. He wasn't so sure now.

His mind was raw. Without Maa nothing was the same. Everything was worse.

Grief – it was shit.

Aamir finished his ice lolly and sighed. He wouldn't have to face Bilal until this evening when his brother came home from work, so he could worry about what he was going to say after he turned up at theirs. In the meantime, he would just hope that Umaira, his kind bubbly sister-in-law, would let him in, serve him a cup of chai, make him meethe chawal – a Mahmood favourite – and let him rest until the axe fell with his brother's appearance.

He would have to wait it out and see what this messed-up day would bring – other than being robbed and bumping into an unusual girl called Mahnoor. She caught his attention, throwing him a furtive glance as she strutted along, her friend by her side. Aamir watched the two of them stroll towards an oak tree that provided plenty of shade for their hush-hush meeting. He wasn't the inquisitive type, but he would have liked to overhear their secretive conversation. The friend stared at him before engaging in a series of wild hand movements. She seemed to be doing all the gabbing while Mahnoor furiously wiped a speck of dirt off her sandals.

Aamir was confident their chit-chat involved him.

Clearly the friend had worked him out.

7
noori

"What are you doing?" Mai grumbled, flapping her arms about in obvious exasperation. "I'm trying to talk to you and you're scrubbing your shoes."

"I'm not scrubbing my shoes," Noori argued, an octave too high. "There was a beetle on my sock. Why do they like white so much? I hate beetles! Is it gone?"

Noori was now shaking her leg, kicking her heel back and forth. She looked ridiculous, but she didn't care. Her beetle phobia had its origin in early childhood, and she preferred not to talk about it.

"Did you see the size of its feelers? They looked like giant fangs!" Noori tried not to screech, and failed.

"Calm down; it's dead," Mai said.

"Really?"

Mai took one sure-footed step forward and squashed the beetle with her platforms: the threat had been eliminated.

Noori shrieked. "You didn't have to kill it!"

"C'est la vie."

Noori squatted down, inspecting the flattened bug. She felt responsible for its death.

"Forget the beetle; we need to talk about that guy," Mai ordered, tossing her head to the side and directing a dismissive glare at Aamir. "Since when have you started hanging out with that lot?"

"What lot?"

"People like him."

"He was sitting on our bench, so I started talking to him."

"Are you bonkers?"

Noori smirked. "You know I am."

"Do you even know who he is? He could be a criminal!"

Noori had to think about that.

"His name is Aamir, he used to play rugby, he likes cricket, and he's into Rumi. Oh, and he faints when he sees blood. Doesn't sound much like a criminal to me."

"Mon amie," Mai said, pouting like a poodle. "I saw the guy this morning on my way to the French bakery, and at first I was like, that *monsieur* is a hunk, but then he stuck his head in the bin and rifled through the rubbish!"

"I don't understand."

"He's homeless and a druggie."

"Nah."

"I'm telling you the truth."

"Just so you know, most homeless people are not drug addicts. And maybe he lost something and was looking for it when you saw him going through the bin."

Mai sighed dramatically, shaking her head. "You're so naive. Didn't you see the bruise on his face? He must duff up people all the time in his drug craze."

"Aamir was the one who was beaten up; he told me."

"Oh, *mon dieu*! Promise me you'll stay away from him. You have no idea who he is, why he's on the streets, and what his motives are."

Noori scoffed. "You make it sound like he's a serial killer."

"You know there's been another attack, here in Clifton," Mai said. "They always target young women or girls. You have to be more careful."

"You talk like my father."

"Speaking of whom," Mai said, adjusting her neckerchief primly. "What's your dad's supposed filthy secret? Is he having an affair? He'd be pretty dumb, because your mum is like *the* most gorgeous woman; but then, it happens all the time. Adultery is pretty common in France, you know."

"My dad's not cheating on my mum!"

"Oh."

"Jeez! Don't look so disappointed." Noori glanced at her feet, trying to find the right words. "He lied," she said quietly.

Now that Noori had the opportunity to vent her anger, she couldn't bring herself to say the words. The truth lodged deep in her throat. Noori could have dealt with her dad having a fling – probably because no one would consider having a fling with him in the first place.

"Lied about what?" Mai asked.

"He doesn't want what's best for me and he's not the person he pretends to be," Noori said. "And now I don't know what that makes him to me."

"Your dad's your dad; that's who he is. And you can't hate him for lying. Everyone's a liar; everyone pretends. The French have a proverb for this; it—"

"Please spare me," Noori groaned.

"Fine. But the French have another proverb for your refusal to be educated, and it—"

"Yes, and we Punjabis also have a saying for this. *Chup!*"

"I know what that means," Mai said with indignation. "You just told me to shut up."

Noori shrugged. "Maybe."

"Rule number one: don't be rude to your friends or you'll end up lonely."

Noori sniffed, taking a moment to ponder loneliness versus aloneness. She wasn't alone. There were plenty of people in her life. She had a family. Parents, siblings, grandparents, aunties, uncles, cousins – other cousins, that is. And while she was part of their tribe, she felt no deep soulmate connection to them. Most of them were just individuals who happened to share certain strands of DNA with her.

That thought didn't help. Shouldn't she find solace in her family, her support system, the people who loved her despite her constant flare-ups? At times she felt so numb, not caring about anyone. It was as if someone had ripped out a giant chunk of her heart. She was slowly bleeding to death and no one was taking any notice. Or maybe they were and Noori was too blind to see, drowning in her pain.

Her sister tried to be there for her. Gentle Zaheera would knock on her bedroom door and ask Noori if she wanted to watch a film, or play that silly video game, or go shopping in Cabot Circus. And each time Noori said no, she could see the crestfallen disappointment in her sister's round, watery eyes. Noori wanted to be left alone and being with her family made her feel lonelier. They didn't get her, and vice versa.

Escaping to Pakistan was the solution because that's where Munazzah was; that's where she could find her cousin and retrace her last steps, and finally say goodbye. Maybe it was dumb, but Noori didn't care. She longed to get out of Bristol, where memories lurked in every corner, ready to pounce. Noori couldn't even lumber up bohemian Gloucester Road without feeling a sharp pinch in her heart. Munazzah had loved the cafes, the graffiti, the independent stores there, always buying her supply of incense sticks in a fair-trade shop.

The last time Noori had ventured into that particular store, the owner had beamed at her, wondering about Noori's absence and casually enquiring about Munazzah. "She's moved away," Noori had lied. It was her way of keeping Munazzah alive, pretending her cousin still existed happily, somewhere, in a distant place.

And that's what she was going to do now. Go to a faraway place. Stay with extended family, attend a private school in Lahore due to her auntie's string-pulling. Naturally, Dad was not happy about Noori's choice to decamp to a distant country.

As if Noori's Pakistani heritage was news to him.

At least she had Mum on her side. Without her mother's support, Noori wouldn't have been able to pursue her master plan. It was Mum who had persuaded Dad, maybe sensing Noori's need to heal, to return to her roots, to look for Munazzah even though she could only be found in tender memories.

She glanced at Mai. Noori would miss her friend. They'd been a gang – Munazzah, Mai and Noori. But Munazzah was gone. And in just over a month Mai was going to start uni to pursue her lifelong dream of becoming a lawyer – she wanted to become the new Amal Clooney. And Noori? Well.

"Oh, look," Mai said, unaware of the turmoil in Noori's head. "The homeless guy is gone."

Noori pivoted and glared at her bench.

It was empty. Aamir had left.

8
aamir

The moment Mahnoor and her friend had turned their backs on him, Aamir had fled the scene like an erratic missile, darting in and out of pedestrians, joggers, dogs and trees. He ended up racing along a wide street, at the end of which he found the Bristol Museum & Art Gallery and a neo-Gothic tower that was affiliated with the local university.

Strange that Mahnoor thought he was a student. Aamir didn't look like someone at uni. He looked like someone on the run, and he was. Under different circumstances he would have liked to go into higher education, following in Bilal's footsteps.

Perhaps he'd get another chance in a year or two. Who knew what might happen in the meantime. Aamir didn't have any big plans for the future. He would just have to go with the flow, follow the road, wherever it might take him. And right now it led him to 7 Park Street, a former sexual health clinic close to the library, right in the city centre.

Cars whizzed past and people did their shopping, unaware that a runaway was in their midst. Aamir stopped, taking in the view, staring at an adulterous couple. They were half naked, one of them hanging from a window ledge, while a third party, a suspicious spouse, scoured the horizon in search of his wife's illicit lover.

Of course, the scene wasn't real. The cheating couple existed as an image, a piece of art graffitied on the wall of number 7 by the famous street artist Banksy. That guy certainly led a double life. He was an enigma, and Aamir liked enigmas. Anonymity had clear advantages, except sometimes being a nobody in a world full of somebodies felt like being part of an empty canvas. And no colour could bring it to life.

Aamir trudged on. He took the long way, going on diversions, passing a little violin shop, lost in his thoughts. Maa had liked Bristol. So had his ex. Claire had talked Aamir into watching a show at the Hippodrome once, a show his brother had also recommended. What were the chances of running into Bilal now, before this evening?

His brother was like Pa in many ways. They held certain beliefs and couldn't be swayed from them. Plus they were both quick to judge when people disagreed with them. Aamir had never told Bilal about Claire, knowing he would ask questions and make assumptions, remind him where he came from. He wouldn't understand – and that was the point. Maa was the only one who had known about Claire, and she had kept Aamir's secret, taking it to her lonely grave.

Now Aamir had to come clean. There was no way round

it. He could traipse up and down Bristol's medieval Christmas Steps all day long, but sooner or later he would have to face Bilal. Aamir knew the route to his brother's harbourside home well now. Every time he came close to Bilal's place, he backtracked. He had passed a snogging couple twice.

It was hunger that drove him there in the end. And the need for some painkillers. His head was still thumping after his involuntary encounter with those crims at the train station. Pa would have referred to them as bandits. And that girl, Mahnoor, she'd called them bullies.

That girl. He couldn't think of a word to describe her other than ... different. He was surprised she'd chatted him up. He didn't exactly look his best. The way her friend had glared at him said it all. It was what made him leave without any explanation. Aamir couldn't stand being judged, especially by strangers. Weird thing was, Mahnoor didn't seem like a stranger, and he didn't think it odd that he was still thinking of her until much later, when he had finally reached his brother's flat and was staring at the bell.

His finger hesitated for a moment before pressing the buzzer. As he lingered outside the block of flats, waiting to be let in, he realized no one was answering the door because no one was home.

Just his luck.

9
noori

"We walked past a Banksy mural with Dad today when he took us to the library," one of the twins announced.

Noori was too lazy to look up from her plate of basmati to see which one it was. Hameer and Zaheera both sounded and looked identical, despite the difference in gender.

Curly-haired and puppy-eyed, the twins were special. They were beautiful creatures, not like Noori at all. As babies they rarely cried, and now that they had hit their early teens, they didn't throw any tantrums. But they were mischievous and nosy AF.

"That's nice," Noori's mum said, adding a heap of yoghurt to the rice. "What mural was it?"

"The adulterous couple," Hameer replied.

"That graffiti sucks," Noori muttered, swallowing a mouthful of rice. "I don't like cheaters, and that couple are big-time cheaters."

"It's supposed to be funny," Zaheera said, trying to keep the peace.

Noori rolled her eyes, then noticed her sister's confused frown and felt mean. She shouldn't be so harsh – the twins were the twins; they hadn't done anything wrong. But she just couldn't stand being around them these days. They demanded too much of her attention. Noori knew they longed to talk to their big sister – about Pakistan, about Munazzah – but Noori avoided them as best as she could. She knew full well how arsey she was acting towards everyone in her family.

They had all noticed Noori's foul mood this evening and had no idea what had caused it this time. She kept mumbling and grunting to herself as she shovelled in forkful after forkful. Being in the presence of her dad didn't help. He had sat there during dinner, making polite conversation with Mum and the twins, acting as if he and Noori hadn't argued this morning. Coward.

"I read an interesting article about Shakespeare today," her father said.

"Shakespeare wasn't that special," Noori retorted, flinging her fork in the air. "And anyway, he was actually a woman."

"Not again," her father said, smirking. "I thought you'd outgrown your conspiracy theory phase."

She glared at him. "Are you afraid to hear the truth, Dad?"

"Mahnoor Marie Oates," Mum said with her Pakistani accent that she'd not been able to shake off despite having lived in England for twenty-seven years. "Calm your temper."

"She definitely inherited that from your side of the family," Dad observed.

"I'm glad I did." Noori was fuming now. "Mum's people had to learn to defend themselves when *your* people invaded *their* lands."

"If you want to go down that colonial route again," her father said, "let me explain that *my* people are also *your* people."

"Only by fifty per cent, and not by choice."

"Mahnoor!" both parents chorused in unison and not in a friendly tone.

She held up her hands. "What?"

Maybe she had gone too far. Blaming her English-born – in other words, white – father for colonial atrocities wasn't exactly fair. Noori was a confused hybrid after all. Half Pakistani, half British, she carried a mixed gene pool and still hadn't learned how to swim in it. But it was time to make a choice. She had to put on her goggles and dive straight in. And at the bottom, maybe she'd find her true self, burrowed deep in a shiny pearl.

She stood up.

"Where are you off to now?" Mum asked, a strange expression on her face. Anger? Her mum was never angry.

"Bedroom."

Noori barged out of the dining room and raced up the staircase into the safe confines of her headquarters. She slumped down on her bed with a frustrated sigh, staring at a picture of Munazzah on the wall. Her cousin had messaged Noori that photo from Lahore, eight months ago, a few hours before she died. She looked beautiful, wearing an airy salwar kameez, the national dress of Pakistan. The blue colour suited Munazzah. She had draped a headscarf over her wavy hair and smiled a toothy smile.

Noori sniffed.

She wasn't going to cry, not now. She was too exhausted to deal with tears. Today had been a weird day. Her argument with Dad, stumbling into Aamir and his tea-stained eyes, getting into yet another fight with her parents – it was all too much.

Her parents knew she was grieving; they were mourning Munazzah's loss too. But the whole family was just acting as if life could go on without her. Mum still trundled to the hospital each day, Dad lectured at the university, Zaheera and Hameer continued to get excellent grades, and Noori slipped into the crack in her heart, Rumi-nating and asking questions that no one could provide answers to.

Minutes, hours, passed. She kept staring at the photograph. There was a twinkle in her cousin's eyes – and that's where Noori found the answer. Every death was followed by a transformation, a rebirth. Noori would show them who she was and what she was made of.

Tomorrow, they'd all be in for a big surprise.

DAY 2

10
aamir

Lying flat on his back with his arms and legs sprawled out on the bench, Aamir remembered a children's book his maa used to read to him about a hungry caterpillar transforming into a beautiful butterfly. He recalled the illustrations, the words, and his mother's tender voice as she brushed a strand of hair from his chubby face.

He gaped at the full moon, waiting for it to smile like it did in the story. But the moon gave him a stony stare, shunning him. Still, Aamir admired its rounded beauty. Nothing could beat the sight of a full moon emerging in the dead of night, bringing light into darkness.

Aamir's eyes strayed to the vastness of the starlit sky and his mind went blank, not a single thought roving around in his head.

Mahnoor.

Damn. It had happened again. Why was he still thinking of her? She had tended to his wound and given him a lolly. Normal people didn't do that.

He tried to redirect his thoughts in an effort to concentrate on something important rather than wasting neurons on a weird girl he didn't know and would never see again.

His brother. Aamir had waited for hours on his doorstep until other harbourside residents started to give him suspicious looks, making him worry they might call the police. That kind of shite happened all the time, especially to people who looked like him.

It made no sense. His brother should have been home. Where else would Bilal spend a Friday evening with his expectant wife? They wouldn't go on holiday now, and even if they had visited friends or gone out somewhere, they would have to come back at some point.

After moving from the doorstep to set up a hideout behind a row of smelly bins, Aamir had watched the comings and goings, studying his brother's neighbours, who all looked the same: professionals, office workers, that type of species. But the parking space reserved for Bilal's car remained empty.

As midnight approached (the thugs hadn't stolen his cheap watch) and the air grew chillier, Aamir realized he had nowhere to go. The prospect of spending the night next to a row of stinky refuse wasn't tempting, especially as he had spotted what was either a scurrying rat or a water vole. And so he had moved on, starving, feeling a constant pain in his head and chest, until he found himself on that bench again, holding on to Maa's picture.

He would have to sleep al fresco tonight. Maybe he came here for sentimental reasons, a sense of nostalgia dragging him back to the past, up the hilly streets. Aamir thought he'd be safe here, for one night at least – but apparently not. He heard the sound of creaking footsteps, of two drunks quarrelling, their slurred words cutting through the crisp night air.

"You're lying!"

"I'm not, you brick!"

"What did you call me?"

The drunkards were coming closer, their voices travelling towards him. Aamir tensed, digging his fingernails into the crumbling paint and holding his breath. If only he had crossed the gorge. He had weighed his options earlier but had decided against trudging over the old suspension bridge that spanned the gorge. What was the river called? It had the same name as those beauty products Maa used to buy. Avon.

Aamir wished he could follow the river, glide above it like a beautiful butterfly, soar over the clayey waterway and muddy banks until he reached its widening mouth. From there he would be able to spot the mighty Severn Bridge that connected Wales with England.

Severn.

That always made him think of *sever*. And that's what he was doing, severing the past from the now. He was an amputee. He could walk, but he had no legs. He could speak, but his tongue made no sense. He had a body, but his soul had become detached.

Aamir wondered what his pa was up to now, on the other side of this river. He'd be asleep, alone in that flat, snoring through the night, maybe worrying about Aamir, feeling guilty for pushing him away. But his father hadn't given him another option. He could never accept that his youngest wasn't like him.

Aamir had always refused to follow his dad's rules. Freedom was what he had craved, and he was paying the price for it now. Who would have believed he'd find himself broke, starving and sleeping rough in Bristol one day? And who would have thought he'd run into a girl named Mahnoor, who had stirred up something unfamiliar in his soupy brain?

He wasn't into her or anything. Aamir wasn't into anyone. Meaningful relationships with people, male or female, meant trouble.

Take that awful thing Claire had said after he returned from his fateful trip to Pakistan. "She'd have ruined your life," she had announced, referring to Maa. What exactly had Claire meant by that? Both his parents were traditional, both had expectations, but Maa would never have done anything to ruin Aamir's life. She wanted her children to be happy, had left her home country to give her kids a head start in life.

Maa hadn't married Pa because she was in love with him – not in the beginning, at least. She had hooked up with him because their families knew each other, had some common relatives, and because he was leaving for France before moving to Wales, where she hoped life would treat them kindly. It's what all immigrants believe, that life can be better elsewhere. Except that's not always the case. The word *sacrifice* popped into Aamir's head. Maa, and even Pa, had given up a lot for their children. Their families, their histories, their land. But what good did it do in the end?

The drunks. He heard them again.

"You think I'm thick?"

"I didn't nick your tenner; you lost it in the club."

"I didn't."

"Hey, wait. What's that over there?"

"A dead dog?"

"No, it's moving."

This couldn't be real. Never had Aamir been thrashed in his life until he had run away from home, and now it looked like he was going to be beaten up twice in twenty-four hours. Was that what they called karma? His blood was rushing in his ears, an internal warning system. He couldn't move. Why was this happening to him? Was it some kind of punishment?

Aamir braced himself, cowering on the bench, listening to their clumsy footsteps. He squeezed his eyes shut, wishing he could beat his butterfly wings and fly away. But he was grounded. They were here now, towering over his foetal body, grinning.

He was in trouble. Again.

11
noori

Ta-da!

Noori gave herself an approving nod in the mirror. She was sporting a rainbow crop top and a pair of harem-style yoga pants, though she neither practised yoga nor lived in a harem, and probably never would. It was a legit outfit, and the scarf would add the finishing touch. Which one should she pick: pink, green or purple?

Pink. A plain silk scarf should do. She stroked the sheer fabric that poured through her fingers like a stream of cool water and gave the scarf a good sniff, digging her trained nose into the delicate material. Noori approved of the smell. Her mum had brought the scarf back from Pakistan and Noori had stored it in a drawer, dumping a bar of patchouli soap on top.

Noori was a sucker for patchouli. She couldn't get enough of that earthy fragrance that spoke to all her senses and reminded her to feel with her inner eye, as Rumi said. Besides, the strong scent was supposed to repel insects, and the same might apply to deceitful family members.

There. She was done. Draped loosely over her head, the scarf made her look like a smokin' badass. There was a bit of hair poking out, a cowlick, but that could be her trademark, her signature style.

Munazzah would have been proud. Maybe.

"Showtime," Noori announced to her smug mirror image, and sashayed down the staircase. It was eight o'clock on a Saturday morning; the whole family should be up by now. Zaheera would be making pancakes in the kitchen; Hameer would be scoffing them; Mum and Dad would be sipping their coffee while reading the paper in the dining room, Dad checking out the sports bit and Mum eyeing the travel section.

Noori burst into the dining room, ready to provoke a reaction, but stopped short: no coffee, no paper, no parents. She traipsed into the kitchen, expecting to see the twins, but again: no Zaheera, no Hameer, no pancakes. Where *was* everyone?

This was beyond annoying. Noori had planned her performance to a T, playing out the scene of her big rebirth in her overactive mind all night. She had practised her entrance ("Morning!"), her body language (subtle brow raise), and her dramatic exit ("See ya!"). And although the general plot stayed the same − Noori entering the room to disrupt her parents' weekend routine − she imagined different scenarios depending on how her parents reacted to the scarf. Whatever the outcome, she couldn't deny the slight rumble of nerves shaking her body.

Her dad wouldn't react well. Oh, he pretended to be a liberal man, married to a South Asian woman whose ancestry was said to date back to some Mughal emperor, but Noori knew better. Her father would eye the scarf with suspicion. His wife didn't wear one, and his kids had been raised to be nonconformists. Faith and religion had never been preached in their home.

Her father's double standards were outrageous. How could the man who had fathered three mixed heritage children have a secret so huge, an agenda so parochial, going against everything Noori stood for? She had to confront him, sooner or later. It wasn't enough to expose him. She had to talk to him before her plane took off to Pakistan.

In six short days she'd be gone, bidding farewell to her family. And when that time came, Noori wanted to be able to look her dad in the eye and let him know what a hypocrite he was. To think the man who had read his children bedtime stories each night when their mum was working a late-night shift, who cuddled them when nightmares plagued their little souls, who let them watch silly cartoons on a Sunday morning even though it was against their mother's rules... To think that man wanted to clip Noori's wings because of what – senility, stupidity, short-sightedness?

Noori swallowed hard. She'd teach him a lesson – one he wouldn't forget. But the more she thought about it, the more she fidgeted with her scarf.

Noori wandered aimlessly around her silent home, waiting impatiently for her audience to appear. She had been up for hours and now her parents were messing with her big moment by having a lie-in. Weren't adults supposed to do stuff on a

Saturday morning? Her parents were getting old. They should be making the most of what time they had left. In fact, they probably wouldn't be able to make it down the stairs soon and would have to install one of those monstrous lifts. Sad.

The sound of the letter box rattling was a welcome distraction. Noori strolled briskly to the front door, pulling a newspaper out of the slot. She skimmed the headlines: the usual crap. Noori grabbed the pen from behind her ear – playwrights always needed one handy – and scribbled her own headline on the front page: "THE BIRTH OF NOORI". She plonked the newspaper on the dining table for her parents to see – once they had rolled out of bed, whenever that might be.

By now her scalp was itching and she fiddled with her headscarf in frustration.

Munazzah had decided to adopt one after her fifteenth birthday. Her decision had taken everyone by surprise, including Noori.

Her cousin had never explained her decision. Munazzah had made it clear it was her personal choice and all she wished was for people to accept that choice. "I can be who I want to be," she had said.

Munazzah had been like that. Interesting, and different. And whatever had motivated Munazzah to wrap a scarf around her head, Noori respected it. And so did everyone else in the family, although some of Munazzah's friends in school were not that chill about it.

Was Noori wearing the scarf to please Munazzah's spirit, or to piss off her dad?

Well, she reasoned, a headscarf was nothing but a piece of clothing, like a hat.

And yet, she felt like an impostor. To be fair, being a hybrid always made her feel like that. She knew her motives were not as pure as Munazzah's; but then again, Noori didn't know *what* her real intentions were. Right now, she only wanted to defy her dad and test his boundaries. She knew something in that wasn't right. But she was angry – nothing else to it.

Noori glanced out of the window. The sky was grey, low clouds dangling over Clifton and its rooftops. She needed fresh air. All this pent-up adrenaline from the abortive Big Reveal had nowhere to go now.

Man, why did she always feel so lost and alone?

She'd head to the park, to her bench, and this time she would remember to grab her handbag. Noori wasn't planning on buying an ice cream today, but you never knew. Maybe she'd bump into Aamir. Yes, the chances were slim, but Noori figured taking *that* chance would increase her ... chances.

She thought about what Mai had said about him. Homeless. A criminal. A druggie. To Noori he was just a guy, and a nice one at that. In fact, if she hadn't given him a lolly and tended his cut, he'd have been helpless. Boys were definitely the weaker sex.

Then he had vanished. He could have said goodbye but ... he was probably embarrassed. Almost-fainting in front of strangers was an awkward affair. Noori had seen him in a vulnerable state and most guys couldn't handle showing their vulnerability to the world. Apparently. Noori shook her head. So dumb.

She marched along, passing some of the park regulars. There was the old uncle, Haqiq, the post office worker, who often took his overzealous beagle for a walk. There was the said young beagle, yapping at a grey squirrel. The squirrel zigzagged its way across the trimmed grass, trying to escape the crazy dog.

Haqiq didn't respond to Noori's cheery "Good morning, Uncle!" He was busy keeping hold of the leash, and when he eventually realized who this bubbly teenager was, he gave a double take. Noori and Munazzah used to amble into his post office every week after school to buy a pack of cinnamon-flavoured gum at one time. Noori *loved* cinnamon-flavoured gum and the post office was the only place in Clifton that sold it.

"Noori Oates, is that you?" he asked.

"Hello, Uncle."

He wasn't her real uncle, but Munazzah had called him Uncle so Noori did too. And Haqiq was a nice uncle. He and his wife had paid Noori's family a visit after hearing about Munazzah. At the time, Noori had watched him wipe a tear from one watery eye. Uncle wasn't afraid of showing his vulnerable side, and Noori appreciated that.

"How are you, *beta*?" Uncle asked, glancing discreetly at her pink headscarf.

Noori was still wondering how to answer that question, and why he referred to her as *beta* – child – when he addressed her again.

"I often think of you and the family," Haqiq continued, pulling the leash and trying to stop the beagle from going after a blackbird perched on a wispy branch. "Your cousin, she had the kindest heart." He sighed. "It's Allah's will; what shall we do? To him we belong, to him we return."

The dog barked, and with one forceful pull it broke free, chasing after the same poor old squirrel. Uncle Haqiq panicked, shouting after his pet as it disappeared behind a row of trees. "I have to go," he said in an apologetic tone before jogging awkwardly after the beagle.

The old man looked funny running after his pet, his voluminous tummy bobbing up and down. Noori half wanted to snigger, but she couldn't. Some things weren't as funny as they looked.

She spotted the bench in the distance. With its scenic vista of the Downs, it was the only place in Bristol where Noori still felt a sisterly closeness to Munazzah. Her cousin had been buried in Pakistan, and Noori didn't attend the funeral. It had all happened so fast, within twenty-four hours of death, as is the custom. Noori should have been there, placing her hands on Munazzah's grave, nourishing the soil with her tears.

Some lines by Rumi popped into Noori's heavy mind.

On the day I die, when I'm being carried
toward the grave, don't weep...
The sun sets and the moon sets, but they're
not gone. Death is a coming together.

A coming together, Noori pondered, as the oak tree came into view and the mad beagle was still yapping. She had almost reached her destination. There was the bench – and what was that thing lying on top of it? A dead dog?

Noori's heart started racing when she realized it wasn't a deceased animal but a human being. She had seen that hoody before.

Aamir.

Now, what were the chances of that?

12
aamir

The good news? He wasn't dead.

The drunks had turned out to be students, only a year or two older than him. After figuring out Aamir was (a) not a dead dog, and (b) not on drugs, they offered him a smoke.

Aamir accepted the offer, although he'd given up smoking after breaking up with Claire. But hey, it was supposed to aid appetite suppression, and it had worked for a bit. Aamir didn't feel as famished now after nibbling on the last few peanuts he had found at the dusty bottom of his backpack. But still he couldn't stop dwelling on food. This, along with Bilal's mysterious absence, was all he could think of. Almost.

Every now and again his thoughts drifted from Bilal's possible whereabouts to Maa's chicken curry to the kindness of strangers. Like the students, or the paunchy uncle with his dog leaving a twenty-pound note on the bench as Aamir pretended to nap. Or Mahnoor, appearing to him in his hour of need.

Maybe the world wasn't as bad a place as Aamir had come to believe. Sometimes good things and good people showed up when he least expected them.

"Hiya," boomed a voice above him. "Didn't think I'd see you again."

"Fu—" he exclaimed, his eyes opening wide in shock. "You scared the hell out of me."

"I don't believe in hell," she said, inspecting him.

That girl, Aamir thought, unable to finish the sentence in his head, distracted by her very weird outfit.

He took a deep breath.

13
noori

Dang it! Mai was right: Aamir was homeless. Why else would he be kipping on the bench on a Saturday morning when half the world were still asleep *in their beds*?

There had been a stunned look of surprise (and embarrassment) when she showed up. It was the second time Noori had found him in a state of vulnerability and it gave her a funny feeling. Was it pity or compassion? She wasn't sure.

Aamir didn't look good. His clammy hair was all over the place, some of it sticking to the crust of the small wound near his temple. He must have dribbled in his sleep; there was a dry trail of spit lining his jaw. A leaf was stuck to his stubbly throat and he took no notice of it.

Some crazy crap must have happened for him to end up on the streets like this. Where was his family? Wasn't there someone looking out for him? It was unbearably sad to think that there were people who abandoned other people.

Noori was intrigued by his situation as much as she was appalled. It was nothing more than curiosity, she told herself. After all, playwrights were curious creatures, interested in fellow earthlings and their fates: the worse the better. OK, that didn't sound right. Perhaps Aamir used to be an addict and his family had kicked him out. Perhaps he didn't have a family. Perhaps he was a thug. No. Aamir didn't look like a ne'er-do-well. He didn't speak like one either. Although, to be honest, Noori didn't know what one would sound like. Either way, Aamir's case probably entailed a bout of bad luck or bad decisions, or both.

After a moment of dazed inaction, Aamir moved gingerly into an upright position, sliding his rucksack off the bench, allowing it to rest next to his feet. Noori slouched down beside him, detecting a different smell today. There was still a trace of pink pepper and musk and magnolia, but there was also an earthy fragrance in the air.

A wild tornado of questions spun around Noori's gusty head. Where did homeless people sleep and get food and water? Did Aamir have any kind of support system, a place where he could go to freshen up, eat something hot, binge on bad TV shows? And when had he last brushed his teeth?

"Gum?" Noori asked finally, producing a strip of her favourite chewy.

"Thanks," Aamir said, hesitating as if he was feeling self-conscious about taking Noori up on her offer.

"How's life?"

Aamir shrugged and Noori inwardly kicked herself. What

an inane question. How did she think someone would feel if they were sleeping on park benches? No wonder he wasn't in an expansive mood. He probably thought she was judging him for being homeless.

"You're not the first guy I've found sleeping on this bench." She laughed nervously. Shut up, Noori! "Last year, my cousin and I discovered a bunch of freshers snoring here. They must have had a wild night partying."

"I wasn't sleeping," Aamir said. His eyes were fixed on the old oak tree.

"What were you doing then?"

"Ruminating."

"That's my favourite word in the world."

Aamir frowned, throwing her a quick glance. "Why?"

"Because of Rumi," she said. "Ruminating with Rumi. You get it, right?"

A hint of a smile flitted across his face. Aamir got it, she thought. What would Munazzah have made of him? Her cousin had been a pro at analysing people. What Noori would perceive to be a person's weakness, Munazzah interpreted as a strength. A flaw, she always said, was a hidden treasure trove. Noori had no idea what her cousin had meant by that, and now she'd never know.

"You look different," Aamir observed, his eyes floating to her scarf.

"Must be my glasses."

"Oh yeah, that's it." He scratched the back of his neck. "They match your headscarf."

Noori ignored the headscarf comment. She was a real queen who didn't care what people made of her.

She was also *such* a liar. Of course she cared.

Aamir gave her a strange stare, as if he had totally sussed her out. She wanted people to notice her new look. She was trying to provoke a reaction so she could feel good about herself; so she could feel real; so she could feel something other than that dark hole in her heart. Noori was copying Munazzah's style but adding her own twist. It might not have made sense to others, but it made sense to her.

"You look different too," she said.

He raised an eyebrow. "That's because I haven't fainted. Yet."

Noori grinned. This guy could actually be funny, and she liked that side of him. She felt the urge to make him smile but why, exactly? She didn't know him, shouldn't care and yet she did. He was a stranger, a desi, yet he wasn't like any of the other ogling desi dudes she had met. He hadn't once mentioned his mum or her cooking, and he didn't try to be cool. He *was* cool.

He was different, and Noori liked different. He didn't act the part, as if he wanted to be someone else. Aamir, she thought, didn't long to be desi at all and Noori couldn't understand why, because that was all she ever wanted, knowing she'd never qualify as a full-blooded native.

With Noori, it was as if someone had mixed milk with mango, softening the flavour of the fruit. She wasn't one or the other. She was different, but not that different. Normal, but not that normal. Noori didn't fit in here or there, but in between: some sort of hyphenated no woman's land that she tried to claim so she could nourish its soil and grow into something bigger than herself.

Where did Noori belong? That question was complex, so complex she gave up on it, and decided to ask another question instead.

"You know the best remedy against fainting?" she asked.

"Nope."

"Chai."

"True."

"Want some?"

Aamir gave her a long, hard stare. This was a definite trait of a desi male. He replied with a head bob.

"Sure," he said.

14
aamir

Mahnoor was full on and Aamir didn't know what to make of her. Like, what was up with the headscarf? She hadn't worn one yesterday, and the way she flaunted it was unusual, ridiculous even.

She really shouldn't wear a headscarf like that, he thought. Did Mahnoor realize what it meant to cover her hair? The cultural implication, the religious symbolism, the stares she would get for ignoring both of these aspects. She couldn't just pick and choose. Choices came with responsibility, Pa always professed, and Mahnoor didn't seem to understand what it meant to wear a headscarf the way his mother had, with pride and reverence, and not with flippant negligence.

None of the women or girls he had come across in his community would have dreamed of combining a veil with a top cropped at the waist. He could see her bare skin, the bulging flesh above her waistband, the line on her spine. It was like she

was mixing styles. Harem pants, sari top, Muslim headscarf –
what was that all about?

Maa would have shaken her head, maybe in amusement.
Did Mahnoor really expect people would take her seriously,
dressed like that? What sloppy message was she trying to
convey? She hadn't thought this one through, that much was
clear. It was as if she was trying to be someone she wasn't.
The girl struck Aamir as confused. Takes one to know one, he
thought ruefully.

But when she had offered him a cup of tea, he couldn't
resist. Chai was chai. Maa would brew it for him after he came
home from a rugby match or a long day at school. And it was
never a treat. It was a staple, a necessity. Aamir hadn't slurped
it in months.

He thought they'd be heading to a tea shop or cafe, and
now that he had twenty pounds in his pocket, thanks to the
old uncle with the errant beagle who'd mistaken him for
a homeless dude, he didn't have to play the role of penniless
vagrant. Mahnoor clearly had her suspicions and it wasn't like
Aamir was trying to fool her, but what self-respecting person
would want the world to know they had nowhere to stay? He
didn't. Even though, technically, he was without a home.

In a way, none of this mattered because, circumstances aside,
how and why was Mahnoor so trusting of strangers? Aamir
never trusted anyone, certainly not any more. Yet Mahnoor
was happily walking beside him with no sign of unease.

"And that's what I mean," she said.

Wait, *what* did she mean?

"Imperialism and postcolonial power structures need to be challenged, one Trump at a time," Mahnoor continued. "Ah, here we go. We've arrived!"

She came to a halt outside a residential home. It was nice: Victorian, three storeys, expensive. It wasn't a tea shop though. Where had she taken him, and how had the time passed so fast? Within the space of a few minutes, she had discussed politics, Bristol's colonial past and slavery, Bollywood, brown feminism, Rumi and mangoes.

He had tried to pay attention to her swerving stream of consciousness, but she skipped from topic to topic so quickly, it was difficult to keep up.

"What's this place?" Aamir asked, pointing at the house.

"My home," Mahnoor said. "You're familiar with the concept of home, right?"

"Not any more."

"How come?" She gave him a puzzled stare, almost stuttering.

"I," he said awkwardly, "don't have a proper home."

Mahnoor frowned at him for a moment. Almost as though she thought he wasn't giving her the full picture. Or didn't believe him. What person didn't have a home? He wasn't a refugee, a migrant on the move, a drifter. She didn't get what it meant to be without a home, without people who made you feel welcome.

Aamir had spent the past eight months living in a two-bed flat in Cardiff with Pa. They'd hardly spoken, let alone talked about Maa's sudden death. Most of the time his father just criticised him. "Why are you not cutting your hair? You look like a fool," Pa had told him on numerous occasions, eyeing Aamir's long mane with distrust. "Are your friends more important than your family?"

Another of Pa's key phrases was "Why are you never home?" On the rare occasion they had sat down together at the kitchen table, the TV was always on, drowning out each other's thoughts.

It was as if they had forgotten how to be around each other without chattering Maa by their sides. She had been the centre of the family; without her, there was no home. Aamir had done the cooking, Dad the washing up. Aamir had been in charge of the cleaning; his father had paid the bills and done the shopping. But was this kind of coexistence homely? Never. It was lonely.

Aamir had preferred to spend most of his time away from that flat and its memories as possible. In the beginning, he fled to Claire's arms, but she made him feel worse, somehow. Pa always asked where he was going, whom he was with, what he was doing, and why he came back late. And Aamir kept lying. Pa didn't understand that Aamir was a seventeen-year-old boy who didn't want to spend a Friday night stuck in a flat that always smelled of Maa's spices, no matter how often you aired the place.

Anyway, it was bound to happen, Pa figuring out what kind of disgraceful son he had fathered. No wonder he had kicked him out. Even if Bilal took him in for a while, he knew it wasn't a long-term solution. There was no quick fix. Aamir had lost his home the moment he lost Maa.

"Everyone has a home," Mahnoor said with resolution, watching Aamir closely.

"I doubt that."

Mahnoor knitted her brows and squinted into the sky as if waiting for someone to descend from the clouds and join her, here on earth. Nothing happened; they just stood there in comfortable silence, like two people who had known each other for an eternity and didn't feel unnerved by each other's muteness.

Her gaze wandered back to him and there was a moment between them – or did he imagine it? He could have easily misread it, yet Aamir was a pretty skilled observer. He'd learned to read people, to copy their behaviour and their language so he could at least pretend to fit in.

The moment was this: Aamir and Mahnoor caught each other's eyes. He smiled, aware he was smiling even though there was no reason to do so. Aamir rarely smiled these days and yet there was something about Mahnoor that lifted his mood. The wonder in her face, the way she had glared at the horizon in awe with admiration or gratitude or … something else?

When she had turned to him, she still carried that soft look, gleaming at him, as though remembering happier times. And there was a second when she transmitted that feeling, whatever it was, to him and he sensed her joy, fleeting as it was. It felt like she was looking at him with fondness though he knew her affection wasn't meant for him. It belonged to someone else, someone close to her heart.

The moment felt weird, intense, stirring up invisible energies between the two of them that drew him towards her, physically. She must have felt it too, because she shifted her stance, taking a step in his direction. And then she spoke in a tone she hadn't used with him before and prodded her index finger – somewhat unwelcomely – into his chest.

"Your soul," she said, "is your true home and you carry it with you wherever you go. Sounds deep, huh?"

Aamir swallowed. "Sort of."

"My cousin came up with that line, not me." Mahnoor sighed and shook her head as if to get rid of an unpleasant feeling. "What did you mean when you said you don't have a proper home?"

Aamir gazed into Mahnoor's chocolate eyes. There was a sprinkle of yellow in them and she looked at him with expectation. He didn't want to lie, but he didn't want to tell her his entire life story either.

"I lost something," he confessed. "A part of me. It makes you question the whole concept of home and stuff."

"What stuff?"

"Life. Like, what's the point of it?"

"Life?" She paused, thinking for a bit. "I guess … the experience is the point of it. Simple."

"It's never simple."

"True. But you can't expect to cruise through life without hitting some obstacles. And who says you have to jump over every hurdle? Sometimes it's worth taking the longer route, going around the obstacle, and eventually you get to the place you want to be." Mahnoor frowned. "That was weird. I don't know where that came from."

Aamir couldn't help but smirk, not that Mahnoor would have noticed. She was watching the clouds again, as if she had travelled to a different galaxy.

"Anyway," she said, "we were going to have chai, so let me get my friend Mai. She'll join us, otherwise my parents will freak."

"Huh?"

"I've never brought a boy home. Definitely not a strange boy, anyway. But they know Mai, so that'll make it OK. Hopefully."

"Wait, we're having chai at *your* house?"

"Yeah." Mahnoor shrugged her shoulders like a Bhangra dancer. "What did you expect?"

"Uh…"

"I'll just get Mai; you wait here."

Mahnoor scooted off to the house next door, ringing the bell of another sizeable Victorian semi that made Aamir feel very small. He needed another smoke. His stomach was cramping, the lack of food squeezing the insides of his intestinal tract, causing his previous nicotine addiction to come back with a vengeance. Maybe Mahnoor would offer him a buttery biscuit with his chai.

Mahnoor's friend flung open the door, shooting him the same horrified look as yesterday. She grabbed Mahnoor and pulled her into the house, closing the door on him. Aamir could imagine part of their conversation, but the part of him that cared started not caring. He was hungry, and thirsty, and if they didn't reappear in the next five seconds, he'd leave and spend his money in a supermarket on some kind of breakfast.

"Noori, I said no!"

The front door banged open and Mahnoor burst out, a phoney smile painted on her face. Her friend followed her.

"Let's go," Mahnoor announced, ignoring Mai, who had fallen silent.

The friend eyeballed Aamir with suspicion as the three of them made their way to the neighbouring house.

"If my parents ask," Mahnoor said, "I'll tell them you're Mai's distant relative, OK?"

"I don't think that's a good idea," Mai protested.

"Nor do I," Aamir added.

"Fear not," Mahnoor said. "We're only having a drink together. What can go wrong?"

And with these fateful words she unlocked her front door and Aamir stepped into Mahnoor's world for the first time. He felt like a fool, jumping blindly off a cliff. But with hunger overwhelming him, his survival instincts kicked in. Nothing else mattered. The chai wouldn't be as good as Maa's, but Aamir hoped it would be decent.

Decent was what he needed.

15
noori

Within a couple of seconds, Noori had gathered all the necessary ingredients and utensils. Full fat milk. Crushed cardamom pods. Cinnamon sticks. Brown sugar. A wooden spoon. Loose tea leaves, which Mum had brought back from her unplanned trip to Pakistan last year, when she had attended Munazzah's funeral.

The chai was now brewing, steaming up Noori's glasses. And Mai and Aamir were gawking at Noori like water bears stranded on the moon. Her guests had not exchanged one word with each other and it was down to Noori to keep the conversation going.

"Biscuits, anyone?" Noori asked.

Mai sniffed loftily. "You know I don't consume refined sugar."

"So you're not having any chai?"

"You know I make an exception for chai," Mai said, adding another superior sniff.

Noori nodded as she looted the cupboard, on the lookout for her beloved ginger nuts. When she discovered them, she tore open the packaging and stuffed a biscuit between her lips.

"Here," she said to Aamir, thrusting the packet into his hands. "Have some. The chai needs another minute or so."

Aamir swallowed, his eyes focused on the ginger nuts. He eagerly pinched a biscuit from the packet and slipped it into his mouth. He took his time chewing that first mouthful, savouring each crumb, and Noori's stomach sank. She should have thought of offering him some food sooner – his fifty-five calorie snack was probably Aamir's first meal of the day.

"Aamir, that's your name, *non*?" Mai asked, narrowing her eyes.

Aamir nodded, still chomping.

"Noori hasn't told me anything about you, like literally nothing. Who exactly are you?"

"I'm a nobody."

"What?" Mai wrinkled her nose, Gallic style. *"Quelle absurdité!"*

"Ouais."

Mai had not anticipated that response.

"Cool, you speak French," Noori said, beaming at Aamir. "You can definitely pass as Mai's relative now."

"Don't be stupid," Mai hissed with contempt. "And I bet he doesn't speak proper French!"

Aamir shrugged. "I was born in Paris," he said.

"So what are you doing in Bristol?"

"Good question."

Noori was thrilled. Paris-born Aamir was a mystery and Noori was drawn to mysteries, the darker the better.

"Morning!" called two voices in unison.

Zaheera and Hameer skidded into the kitchen, followed more sedately by Noori's parents, who did not immediately register that there was a new face, or a pink headscarf, present in their home.

"Didn't get a wink of sleep last night," Noori's yawning dad said.

"You're telling me," Mum replied, sounding a bit disgruntled.

"Must have been the full moon," Hameer added.

"Kept me up all night," Zaheera said.

"It's the gravitational force."

"I know. It messes with our subconscious and stuff."

"Have you heard about the water bears that have crash-landed on the moon?"

Suddenly the twins came to a halt, Hameer bumping into Zaheera. They were the first to spot Aamir and then the novel headscarf.

"You're late," Noori pointed out. "It's half past ten."

"Hang on," her father said, pointing a hairy finger at his eldest daughter. "What is that?"

Noori wasn't sure whether he was referring to the headscarf or Aamir. She decided to concentrate on the latter first.

"This is Aamir," she said brightly. "He speaks French. I mean – he's one of Mai's distant cousins."

Mai's mouth twitched and Noori knew she was pushing

her luck. Aamir bit into another ginger nut, smiling without smiling, greeting Noori's family in his chill-pill way. How could he be so cool all the time?

Mum took a step forward, her watchful gaze taking in the sight of a headscarf-donning Noori before moving on to Aamir.

"Hi," she said to him, "nice to meet you."

The twins, quiet all of a sudden, murmured a "Hi there" while her double-faced dad mumbled something inaudible under his breath. Out of all the people present in the room, Mai looked the most uncomfortable. She was acting like she had a colony of ants in her pants and was keeping an eye on the exit.

"Why don't we, uh, go and have our tea in the conservatory?" Mai asked Noori.

"Sure. You two go ahead. I'll pour the chai; will be there in a sec," Noori said.

"But…"

"I bet you cousins have a lot of catching up to do. Off you go!"

Mai shook her head. This would cost Noori. She would have to trade her baguette-shaped earrings for her friend's silent compliance.

It was obvious Mai did not want to leave without Noori, as if she was afraid of being alone with Aamir. Noori gave her friend a gentle shove and watched her disappear through the swinging kitchen door. Aamir tagged along, still clutching the pack of ginger nuts.

"Mai's cousin looks like that actor," Zaheera whispered to her twin once Aamir was out of earshot and the family were on their own, busying themselves with preparing breakfast and staring at Noori's headscarf every now and again. Noori was straining the chai, and her ears. Dad was mumbling something to Mum, and Noori tried to guess who would be the first to comment on her pink scarf.

They all believed Noori had to be handled with care, as if there was an invisible "FRAGILE" sticker stuck to her forehead. "She's out of sorts," Mum had said a few weeks ago after Noori had announced she was going to go vegan, even though she loved lassi, and fish and chips.

When Noori had trudged home one afternoon flaunting a nose stud, her parents were ambivalent. Mum *seemed* to like it. She used to wear a nose piercing but had removed it once she entered the medical profession. And Dad hadn't said a word. He was a historian, seeing repeating patterns everywhere. He analysed the era of Noori like any academic by coming up with random theories.

Noori filled up three glasses of chai and plonked them on a shiny tray. She had come to the conclusion that Hameer would be the first to comment on her headscarf. She was right.

"Noori," her thirteen-year-old brother said, blunt as ever. "Why are you wearing that thing on your head?"

"Funny. Mai asked me the same question."

"Is it a joke?" her father chirped in, sounding like an angry bird. "You can't be serious."

"Whatever."

"Don't whatever me."

"Then don't patronize me."

"I'm not patronizing you; I've asked you a question and you haven't answered."

"OK, here's my answer."

They all waited, the twins looking on with curiosity, Noori's parents blinking at their daughter in quiet anticipation.

Nothing happened.

Noori's silence was her answer, but they didn't get it. Nobody got Noori these days. The world had turned upside down and Noori didn't know how to move it downside up.

Her best friend was gone.

And she was getting flashbacks all the time. Out of the blue Noori remembered the moment they had said goodbye on the day Munazzah headed to Heathrow with her parents to catch their flight to Lahore. Her cousin had pulled her in for a cuddly hug that lasted forever. It was like she didn't want to let her go.

"I'm going to miss you, baba," Munazzah had said.

And Noori had laughed, asking why. "It's only two weeks," she had protested.

It transpired that Noori was wrong. Those two weeks had turned into a lifetime. How could she live this life without Munazzah, her soulmate, the only person who could make sense of Noori when Noori couldn't make sense of herself?

Noori would have liked to weep right there and then in front of her mismatched family, but instead, head high and heart breaking, she strutted off to the conservatory, balancing three cups of chai on the tray.

Her special guest was waiting.

16
aamir

"Just so you know," Mai said with hostility, "I've seen you before."

Aamir nodded. "Yeah, we met yesterday."

"That's not what I'm talking about." She clicked her tongue in disgust. "I mean, I've *seen* you before."

Aamir also had an uncomfortable feeling of having met Mai before. But this was only his second day in Bristol and so far he had spent most of his time avoiding human contact. It was what runaways did. But now he had become acquainted with Mahnoor, dodging people seemed impossible.

"I know you've got something to hide," Mai said accusingly. "You disappeared without a trace yesterday, didn't you? Only crooks do that sort of thing."

"A crook." Aamir smirked. "Do people still use that word?"

"Noori does." Mai sniffed, her gaze narrowing as she munched another ginger nut.

"Fine, call me a crook then."

"I knew it! And I bet you weren't born in Paris."

"If you say so."

"Look," Mai said. "You might fool Noori, but you can't fool me. The only reason I'm talking to you is because Noori is my friend and I need to protect her from herself because she's *not* herself. It's crazy to pick up a random guy from the park and offer him chai! And now the headscarf thing. You see what I'm trying to say here? Noori's *grieving*. Her cousin died, so stay away from her." She paused. "I mean, that's none of your business, but I mean it. Stay away from my friend."

"Oh, looks like the distant cousins are getting on at last," Mahnoor said before Aamir could react, strolling into the conservatory and placing three cups on the table. "What have you guys been chatting about?"

Mahnoor settled into a seat next to Mai and started slurping her chai. She sighed in bliss.

It must be good, thought Aamir and grabbed his cup. The moment his lips touched the spicy liquid, his taste buds started fizzing.

Unbelievable. This was almost as good as Maa's.

Mai flushed. "We weren't talking about anything that mattered," she said defensively.

"You were having a go at Aamir," Mahnoor said. "I heard you."

"I wasn't. I just told him to bugger off."

Mahnoor eyeballed Mai.

"I mean it," Mai said. "He can finish his tea, but then he has to leave."

"Since when are you sending people out of *my* house?"

"I'm just trying to…"

Mahnoor stared meaningfully at Mai. There was some serious non-verbal communication going on, and Aamir didn't stand a chance of figuring it out. Girls and their secret languages. It looked like it was a stand-off. Mahnoor didn't seem like she would be the one to budge; eventually her friend glanced away first.

Aamir thought about Mai's comment. Could she be right? Perhaps Mahnoor really wasn't herself. Grief was a strange thing. He knew all too well it made people lose their way.

"So, Aamir," Mahnoor said, smiling at him, and there was something unnerving about that toothy grin. "You were born in France, but you said you were British."

"Yeah."

"How come?"

"Turned out that way."

"Interesting."

"There's nothing interesting about that!" Mai snapped, swigging down the chai. "My mum was born in Vietnam, grew up in Oslo, moved to France and became a naturalized citizen before marrying a Scot whose parents had migrated from Sicily."

"Yes, and that *is* an interesting story," Mahnoor agreed. "It would make an intriguing play or film."

Well. Aamir was in the wrong movie. How had that happened? Oh yeah, it happened because he had decided to run away from crazy people only to end up with more crazy people.

Wasn't life ironic. The chai was excellent without a doubt, but the friend was right. The moment he'd emptied his cup, Aamir would leg it.

"What're you looking at?" Mai asked him.

"He's looking at a butterfly," Mahnoor said. "It's beautiful, isn't it?"

It was magnificent. The little blue butterfly had found a sunny spot on the windowpane, flapping its wings every now and again. Butterflies were all about transformations and building cocoons. Maybe Aamir was in the middle of making his own cocoon, without realizing it.

Aamir's arbitrary thought pattern was interrupted when Mahnoor's mother entered the room, flying into the conservatory without making a sound.

"Zaheera is making pancakes – would you like some?" she asked in a thick accent that reminded him of Maa.

"Yes, please," Mahnoor said.

"No, thank you, not for me," Mai said. "I have to leave, and this guy – he has to leave too."

"Oh," Mahnoor's mother said, "maybe next time?"

"We'll see."

"Why don't you and your cousin come around for lunch tomorrow, before you head off to the airport? There's time, isn't there?"

"That's kind, but—"

"Shame on you, Mai," Mahnoor interrupted. "You know you're mortally offending my mother by turning down an invitation to lunch."

It was true. Her mother seemed both offended and annoyed, frowning at Mahnoor's weird friend. Aamir knew that reproachful look, had seen it a million times on Maa when she insisted on cooking a three-course meal although he had only asked for a glass of water.

"Think about it," Mahnoor's mum said with the classic authority of a mother.

"But—"

"You think about it, and I shall expect you and your cousin at one o'clock sharp."

And with these words Mahnoor's mother gave Aamir a mysterious smile and floated out of the room. The mum was nice; he liked her. The shiny black hair, the sing-song voice, the accent, the gold bangles on her wrist. She was familiar.

"OK, time to go," Mai announced, finishing her drink. "And you, *cousin*, are coming with me."

She spat out the word *cousin* and barged out of the conservatory. Aamir would have liked to savour the final sip of chai, but he ended up gulping it down. The sooner he left, the better.

Mahnoor didn't try to stop them; she just shrugged her shoulders and followed. They didn't pass any of her family on the way, and Aamir thought that was for the best. After today, he'd never see them again.

He felt Noori's eyes on his back, turning his head once to catch her staring straight at him. During that brief moment, when she didn't expect to be seen, he caught a glimpse of something he knew all too well. Sadness.

No words were spoken until the three of them had darted through the front door and gathered outside Mahnoor's house next to a row of recycling bins. Mai grabbed Mahnoor's elbow, whispering something in her ear. Like yesterday, the two were having some kind of heated debate.

Aamir threw Mahnoor one final glance. How had he missed her grief before? She was good at hiding things. Maybe that was why she was wearing the headscarf, as camouflage.

Aamir should have thanked Mahnoor for the chai before disappearing out of her life, and for good this time. Maa had raised him to be a polite boy, a good son, but her efforts had been thwarted. Aamir wasn't a good son.

And he wasn't a good person, not any more.

17
noori

There's a simple way to heal a broken heart.

Step one: locate pain.

Step two: feel pain.

Step three: let said pain go.

How? By allowing healing light to enter the crack in your heart. But how was Noori supposed to find this magical source of light? Should she engage in topless sunbathing, shine a love-scented candle on her heart space, or find a celestial torch made of starlight? She had tried everything, including listening to Tibetan zen music, but nothing had worked.

Noori was alone in the conservatory, thinking about pain and suffering, and the difference between the two. One was curable (suffering), the other one (pain) wasn't. Pain was necessary to survive; suffering crushed any hope of survival. That sounded satisfyingly deep, and she wanted to share the thought with someone, but nobody was around.

Mai had left after lecturing Noori about strangers like Aamir. "He could be a pimp!"

Noori had given her friend an incredulous stare, at which point she realized Aamir had vanished. If there was one thing he excelled at, it was running away. Noori wanted to feel angry – she had invited him in for chai and then he'd done a runner. Was that the way to thank her? But the weird thing was, she didn't feel her usual anger. She just felt left behind.

Her father strolled into the conservatory holding a plate of pancakes topped with lemon juice and honey, her favourite.

"Here's your order," he said, adding a tight smile.

Noori fake-smiled back. "Thanks."

She took a savage bite of pancake, a trickle of sticky juice running down her chin. It was nice of Dad to offer her comfort food when she was in need of comfort. Maybe he could sense her desolation.

And maybe this was a good time to talk. It was just the two of them. If she were to confront him now, nobody would overhear them. Nobody would know. The twins had retreated to their rooms to play their dumb video game. They had asked Noori to join them, probably as an excuse to quiz her on the headscarf or Aamir, but Noori had turned down their invitation as usual. And Mum was on the phone to her mum. Their calls could last hours.

Still, Noori hesitated. How should she approach the topic? It wasn't easy to expose her father's secret in front of her father. It was far easier to argue about meaningless things instead. Noori chewed it over, munching on her pancakes. Dad had used her favourite honey, the dark one. He knew her taste and yet clearly he didn't know anything else about her.

"Five days," Dad said, more to himself. "Are you sure going to a Pakistani school is what you want?"

"No comment."

She'd had this type of discussion before, like a million times, and every time he said the same things, and she said the same things, until she ended up hissing at him and storming out of the room. The way he pronounced *Pakistani school* like it was inferior to her current British school caused her blood to boil. She was, after all, half Pakistani, and what was second-class about that?

"Where are your friends?" he asked, as if he had only now noticed that the two of them were on their own. That man ... so blind.

Noori continued stuffing her face. "Gone," she mumbled.

"I have to say, Mai's cousin doesn't look at all related to her."

"I don't look related to you, and yet I'm your daughter," Noori retorted, giving her father a look of reproach.

That was the other thing. Noori and her father bore little resemblance to each other. People took one look at her skin, compared it with her father's, and never guessed the two were related. In fact, Noori didn't look like either of her parents. It had been commented on more than was polite, and even she couldn't quite understand how her parents' gross baby-making had produced someone like her. The twins were different. They had inherited Dad's distinct nose and were gifted with their mother's high forehead. Noori paid attention to these details

97

and, in a way, she was glad she didn't resemble her parents. She wanted to be her own person. But still. It didn't always help her feel less alone.

Noori glanced at her dad. Why did he look like an injured deer that had been shot by Noori's arrow? She didn't want to feel sorry for him. He had betrayed her. No. He had disappointed her. Dad was a chameleon and she'd seen his true colours.

"Noori," he said gently. "I know it's not been easy." Noori grunted in response, which he took as permission to continue talking. "Can't you see we're all in this together? I want to understand—"

"What, Dad?"

Noori dropped her plate, giving her father another hard stare. He was gazing at her as if he didn't recognize his daughter. She was challenging him, provoking him, waiting for him to comment on her headscarf again so she could vent her anger at him. And he, unwittingly, complied. His eyes wandered to her pink scarf.

"Munazzah wore a hijab," he said.

Silence.

"Is that why you've put it on?"

"You make it sound like I'm committing a sin."

"Of course not, but when you think of what it means… Just look at what happened in the Middle East—"

Noori cut him off. "I'm not in the Middle East, and it's fine if someone doesn't want to wear a headscarf, but it should also be OK if someone else does. No one is forcing me to do anything; I have free will. People can wear whatever they want; it's not like I'm telling you off for wearing a sun hat or your stupid Chewbacca mask."

"You can't compare the two."

"Says who? The man who thinks he can control my life?"

"What is that supposed to mean?"

"I'm giving you a tip, Father. I know what you did. I know about that *secret* phone call."

He looked blank. "Haven't got the foggiest what you're talking about."

"You never do."

"Why are you always running off when I'm trying to talk to you?" Noori heard Dad say as she grabbed her plate and cruised to the door.

She couldn't stand being around him. It was no man's business if a woman, or a girl, wanted to wear a headscarf. This was part of *her* heritage, not his. She'd always felt different, *was* different, and the headscarf accentuated her inherent otherness, which she was trying to embrace and understand.

Was it extreme to wear a headscarf all of a sudden without understanding what it truly signified? Probably. But Noori was old enough to make her own choices, the way Munazzah had. She was a new person, a new Noori, and if she wanted to wear a headscarf, she'd wear a headscarf. If she wanted to invite a strange boy home because she liked him, hell yeah, she'd go ahead and do just that.

Not that she'd ever see Aamir again.

Mai was right: Aamir should have buggered off sooner and not wasted Noori's precious time. Why did she feel so drawn to him anyway? Because he had kind eyes? Nope. She had liked him because he reminded Noori of her favourite Bollywood actor, Mister Kapoor, in his role as a crazy drug addict and rock star, facing the end of his career. And in the film, Kapoor's character redeems himself by saving a girl from a bunch of pimps after she saves him first.

But Aamir, the boy who didn't understand the concept of home, was no Mister Kapoor. He was a nobody.

Like Noori.

DAY 3

18
aamir

Aamir had lost the twenty-pound note. He had frantically searched every pocket and every crack, retracing his steps on the lookout for the money. The only thing of value he came across was a small Swiss army knife that lay abandoned on the pavement. Aamir picked it up – a knife could always come in handy.

Day three in Bristol and Aamir was still broke, starving and clueless as to how to get out of this messy situation – unless he robbed a bank, threatening the employees with a miniature knife.

What on earth was he thinking?

And just where the F was Bilal?

Perhaps he should turn himself in, ramble to the next police station and ask to use the phone so he could make one call and put an end to all of this. Pa would pick him up, or maybe he wouldn't. Aamir had brought shame to his family and been told what a useless son he was. Unless he reformed his character, Pa would never take him back.

It had been in one of *those* moments, when he had reached his lowest low and his father had found him curled up on the bathroom floor three days ago, that Pa had spoken the hurtful words. "You're not my son. No child of mine would behave like that." And then he'd preached about Allah, and when Aamir in his drunken state slurred "Fuck your God!" his father quietly closed the door on him. The last thing he'd said to Aamir was this: "Leave my house when you're sober. And don't think of coming back until you're right in the head."

And here he was, sleeping rough on benches, seemingly tethered to Bristol, which would not catch him a break. If he went back to Cardiff he could stay with one of his rugby mates for a few days, and work out his next steps. Aamir might risk running into Pa or Claire then, but at least he'd have a roof over his head and some food in his sinkhole of a stomach.

Realistically, all options still led back to his brother. Aamir would just have to beg Bilal to take him in. He'd give it one more day. Presuming Bilal and Umaira had gone away for the weekend, they would return today, Sunday. And if they didn't, he'd hitch a ride back to Cardiff.

His tummy rumbled again.

Mahnoor's mum had invited him and Mai for lunch today. One o'clock sharp, she had said. Aamir would forsake his dignity for a decent lunch and another cup of chai. He couldn't believe he was actually considering it. When had he become a sponger living off other people's good will? His father was right. Aamir was a loser, and with his attitude, he'd never make it anywhere in the world.

"One step at a time," Maa used to say.

Maa.

What would she make of him now? All the trouble she had gone through, raising two boys in a strange country, trying her best to turn them into honourable young men. She had succeeded with Bilal, while Aamir had always been the troublemaker, smoking in secret, drinking in secret, dating in secret.

"Don't tell your father about Claire; he won't understand," Maa had told Aamir when she found out about his ex. He'd felt such a huge sense of relief. Aamir had believed Maa to be his accomplice, someone who understood his feelings. He had liked Claire at the time, enjoyed being with her, in the beginning. And Maa didn't scold him for choosing a girl who wasn't from their community, as she used to phrase it.

It wasn't until their Pakistan–India trip that the penny dropped. Bilal had just got married and the Mahmoods were making their rounds, visiting people Aamir had never heard of: pot-bellied men plus their middle-aged wives and their pretty offspring. Girls his age were giving Aamir inquisitive looks. Some were Muslims; others were Sikhs; none of them tried to speak to him. But they giggled, flitting in and out of the richly decorated living rooms to check him out.

Afterwards Maa had joked about them. "Those girls were nice. I think Saira fancied you."

"The one with Wolverine sideburns?"

"Aamir!"

"Ouch! Why did you smack me?"

"You treat women with respect, you hear me?"

"I know that, all right?"

"Good." She paused to give her youngest son a kiss on the head where she had just knocked him. "I don't want you complaining about my future daughter-in-law, sideburns or no sideburns."

"I'm not planning on getting married. Ever."

"Don't be silly." Maa smiled. "Look at Bilal; he couldn't be happier now we've found him a wife. And when you're older, we'll do the same for you."

"But—"

"Don't worry. First, you go to university and finish your studies. Then we'll see. One step at a time."

And that's what Aamir was doing, taking one step at a time, shuffling along unfamiliar roads, his legs taking him places he'd never been. Like the Bristol Museum & Art Gallery. He could refill his water bottle there, brush his teeth, and rinse his face so he'd look and smell less like a stray poodle. And then? He'd see where his next step would take him.

One thing was for sure: he had to find Bilal. And soon.

19
noori

"What's your mum cooking for lunch?" Mai asked, trying to zip up a suitcase that was brimming with unnecessary stuff like four pairs of flip-flops, five bathing suits and bikinis, six bottles of perfume, and a waffle maker. Mai loved her daily breakfast dose of sugar-free waffles and she never travelled anywhere without her waffle maker. Not even to the South of France, where Mai and her parents were about to enjoy two weeks by the sea.

"You think she's making samosas?" Mai asked.

"Don't know."

"I love your mum's samosas."

"I know."

"I don't have to be at the airport until five so there's time, you know, to have a proper farewell feast," Mai said, ramming her knee into the suitcase in an effort to squash it and close the zip. "I won't see your family for a couple of weeks, and then I'm off to uni, and you'll be in Pakistan, and who knows when I'll be able to hang out with my favourite neighbours again."

"You're going to study law here in Bristol; it's not like you're moving to the other side of the world."

"But it won't be the same. You won't be here, and I might not have the time to pop in and—"

"Scoff Mum's samosas."

"Yeah, that's what I'm saying."

"You're expected for lunch anyway, so stop talking about it."

"And what if your parents ask me about my distant relative? It's odd if I'm showing up without that weirdo, *non*?"

"Who cares? You're used to lying to parents, so you'll come up with something."

"You're right. I'm a superb liar."

Noori fell into a moment of silence. She hadn't thought about Aamir until Mai had brought him up. Truth was, Noori felt childish and immature about her behaviour. Why had she invited Aamir home, and what was it about him that made her want to open up about stuff?

All that talk about the concept of home and the meaning of life – it seemed mad that she'd discussed these things with him when Munazzah had been the only one privy to her random thoughts. And then Aamir had vanished without saying goodbye, leaving Noori embarrassed and disappointed.

"I wonder how he is," Noori said now.

"Who?"

"Aamir."

Mai took a deep breath. Noori could smell her friend's thoughts. Either she was going to shout and start talking about pimps again, or she'd pretend not to have heard her. Mai would make a scary lawyer one day.

"Will you stop thinking about him!" Mai ordered, flaring her nostrils.

"He needs help. Everyone who doesn't get the meaning of life or the concept of home needs help."

"OK, and while we're at it – why don't we let him stay at my place?" Mai laughed a fake laugh. "He can have the whole house to himself when I'm on holiday, and maybe he'll get the concept of home then!"

Noori rolled her eyes. Mai could be so cold sometimes. Her ex-boyfriend had turned her into a cynic. That guy was an arse, but for some reason Mai had ended up wasting one year of her life with him until he ditched her via text. And, ever since, Mai had taken a dislike to good-looking males, suspecting them of being cheating idiots. Aamir was no exception.

"You have to admit one thing," Noori said. "Aamir's easy on the eye."

"*Pff!*" Mai had finished packing and sat down on her suitcase, giving Noori a disconcerting stare. "I don't want to hear another word about him. Let's talk about you instead."

Noori felt a tremble in her heart. She hated it when Mai used her "let's talk about you" phrase that she had come to adopt since Munazzah's death. Noori didn't want to chat about herself or her feelings.

There were certain things Noori didn't discuss. This

included but was not restricted to all private and confidential details about her life. The only person she had discussed these matters with was Munazzah. And now that her cousin was dead, Noori engaged in personal conversations with Rumi. If Munazzah had believed in his advice, why couldn't Noori – even if he was a bloke and probably didn't get things like headscarves, or PMS, or childbirth.

"Are you excited about your trip? Have you packed your stuff? And what about your dad?" Mai asked. "Are you going to tell me his secret or not?"

"Is this a cross-examination under oath or what?" Noori laughed nervously, trying to gulp down her spit. "I packed my stuff ages ago, to answer one of your hundreds of questions. And Dad's taking me to the airport, which should be interesting. I can't believe it's only four more days."

"I know," Mai said, lowering her eyes. "I'm going to miss you and your clever ways of not answering my questions."

"I have answered them."

"Not all of them. What's this sin your dad's committed, which is *so* bad?"

"I don't want to talk about Dad now," Noori said resolutely.

There was an awkward pause in their conversation and Mai gave her that weird look.

"You know, Noori. Sometimes…" There was a bit more hesitation. "Sometimes you can be a bit mean. Your dad only worries about you," Mai said, her gaze flitting to Noori's headscarf.

Mai always tried to act like the old and wise one when she

wasn't. That had been Munazzah's role. And Mai was far from reaching that state of enlightenment.

Noori thought to the future. Once she was in Lahore, amongst strangers, she could forget her woes for a bit and pretend she was less like her current self. Maybe she could even come to some sort of acceptance of Munazzah's senseless death, when she saw for herself where it had all happened, and where she'd been laid to rest. Maybe she would find peace, the way Munazzah had.

"It's because of Munazzah, isn't it?" Mai now asked, giving Noori her undivided attention.

Noori feigned ignorance. "What are you waffling about?"

"The headscarf. Munazzah wore one."

"Everybody thinks that everything I do is because of her."

"No, that's not what everybody thinks," Mai said carefully. "But you avoid talking about her and push us all away."

Noori wanted to deny everything, but Mai had broached a subject she couldn't ignore. Noori knew she found it difficult to let people in these days. She even cringed whenever Mum pecked her on the cheek. She was totally unable to handle human closeness. Even watching a Bollywood film with the twins felt weird, because Noori preferred to stare at the screen alone, so no one would see the raw emotions scribbled on her face when the lovers didn't end up together, or the tragic hero died trying to save the world single-handedly.

Her self-imposed isolation had become a pattern she hadn't been aware of in the beginning. Noori had drawn an invisible boundary around herself and whenever somebody approached its fringes, she built a wall, ready to battle anyone who dared to invade her territory.

Sometimes Noori wondered what would have happened if Munazzah had lived and Noori had died. How would her cousin have handled Noori's death? Would she have abandoned or turned to her God? Noori found it difficult to think of a deity without questioning its existence. And yet here she was donning a headscarf which was laden with religious meaning.

"How can you be so sure God exists?" Noori had asked her cousin once.

Munazzah, who had been in the middle of painting her nails purple, looked up and lazily shrugged her shoulders. "That's a moron question."

"I'm serious; tell me," Noori had begged.

"Baba," Munazzah had said. "It doesn't matter why I believe in God; the question is: why are you asking me?"

Munazzah had had a knack for turning conversations around, never wanting to make things about herself. She was more interested in learning about other people and what made them tick.

There was this thing she had told Noori on the day she was due to fly out to Lahore. "You know why I love you?" Munazzah had asked Noori, as they were slurping their last lassi together. Noori rolled her eyes, thinking her cousin would come up with a dumb explanation like "Because you're a moron." Instead, Munazzah had grabbed Noori's hand and said: "You're always you. You're never who anyone expects you to be."

As if on cue, Mai spoke. "You have to admit, *mon amie*,

you've not been yourself lately." She watched Noori unwrap a strip of chewing gum.

Mai was right, and of course Noori appreciated their friendship. And since Mai had been friends with Munazzah, she missed her too. But their bond was different. Munazzah and Noori were bound by blood and years of companionship. They could chat for hours, or sit in silence, not doing anything. If there was one person Noori had relied on one hundred per cent, it was Munazzah. But it turned out Noori should have relied on her cousin ninety-nine per cent. That would have saved her one per cent of heartache.

As Noori sat in ponderous silence, Mai sighed. "I'll be here when you need me, when you want to talk," she said softly. "I'm one call away. Always."

Noori wanted to throw her arms around Mai right there and then. A big part of her wanted to believe in Mai. But Munazzah had said the same and that had been a lie. Nobody should make promises they couldn't keep.

"Shall we head over now? It's almost one o'clock," Mai said.

"I thought you wanted to take Doughnut out for a walk first."

Doughnut, at hearing his name, stirred in his pillowy nest, pointing his squidgy ears upwards. He was the dumbest dog Noori had ever met, but he was adorable, and a beagle. What were people's obsessions with beagles?

"Yeah," Mai said. "Let's take him for a walk, next door. He needs to get used to you guys since you'll be the ones looking after him in my absence."

"He's known us, like, forever."

"Still. He's more sensitive than you think."

Mai whistled for Doughnut and the dog trotted towards his owner, licking Mai's bare feet. Gross. This dog had a foot fetish. He was obsessed with sniffing people's socks, hoofs and loafers.

Doughnut wagged his tail in anticipation as Noori and Mai made their way next door. Doughnut had, of course, been Munazzah's pet. But after her death, Noori's uncle and aunt had filed for divorce and nobody wanted to keep the beagle. Hence Mai had adopted him. She loved that dumb dog, and the dumb dog loved her.

Despite Mai's worries, Doughnut always felt at home with Noori and her family. He snuggled down in his favourite spot in the conservatory, the papasan, and promptly fell asleep. Noori was all alone with him now, watching him scratch his cheek in his sleep.

Mai had joined Mum in the kitchen, no doubt pinching food while pretending to help. Dad was outside doing the gardening, pruning and snipping away, unaware of Noori's watchful eyes. She couldn't help remembering when she used to dig up plants with him. The twins were doing their twin thing: staring at their phones somewhere in the depths of the house, seeking moments of solitude. Much like Noori.

Yesterday Noori had sat here with Aamir. He had munched ginger nuts and drunk his chai as if all was well in the world, when it clearly wasn't. Why was he sleeping in a park? Where were the people who loved him? Had he betrayed his family, or vice versa? There were so many important details Noori was desperate to know.

"*Gah* – forget him!" Noori blurted out loud.

Doughnut winced in his sleep as Noori spoke. Maybe Mai was right and the dog had more brains than she gave him credit for. He definitely possessed some kind of sixth sense. It used to freak Noori out, like he'd start barking and racing to the door a good five minutes before Munazzah had even arrived at the house – at least that's what she'd been told.

And then there was this thing that had happened on the day Munazzah died, when Doughnut had been snoozing in Noori's room. Munazzah and her parents had travelled to Pakistan over the Christmas holidays, so of course the dog had stayed with her. He'd been quiet all night, but then at five twenty-eight in the morning he'd started howling and weeping. The tears in his eyes still haunted her. Two hours later, they'd received the phone call.

The dog had known Munazzah was gone long before Noori did.

Noori jolted out of her seat as the beagle woke up and, without giving any prior warning, did his weird yapping thing. "Bloody hell, you dumb dog!" she gasped, close to a heart attack.

Doughnut barked in excitement, rushing past Noori out of the conservatory to the front door, as if expecting Munazzah to knock.

"Come back!" Noori shouted as she followed him. "Munazzah's gone."

That came out more bitterly than she intended.

Doughnut paid no attention to Noori, but instead headbutted the front door repeatedly.

Maybe he needed to poop. Noori hated dealing with dog poop. Where was Mai, his rightful owner? It looked like he couldn't keep it in any more. Did dogs get diarrhoea? She had to get him out before he made a mess of her parents' Nepalese rug.

"OK," Noori said. "I'm sorry, I misunderstood you. There, you can go now."

She swung the door open, expecting Doughnut to flash through it, but he didn't move an inch. The dog's dilated pupils were fixed on the person standing on the porch.

It was none other than Aamir. Again.

20
aamir

"Ever thought of taking up a career as a magician?" Mahnoor asked in a snappy voice.

"Um, no," Aamir said, unsure.

"Well, maybe you should. You've got an uncanny knack of disappearing and reappearing."

She didn't sound happy, that much Aamir could tell, but she didn't sound unhappy either. At first, Mahnoor just gaped at him in total disbelief, her chocolate eyes expanding into two shiny buttons. She let out a whistle, which Aamir interpreted as her way of showing mild discontent. But then he realized she was addressing the dog, not him.

"Doughnut, come here," she commanded like a general on the front line.

The dog, quite an old one by the look of it, didn't move. It gazed up at Aamir for one brief moment and then decided to settle its head on his shoes. And that's where it stayed, making whiny noises and every now and again giving Aamir's trainers a slobbery lick.

"Come on, you need to move," Mahnoor said. "You can't lie on top of people's feet all the time." The dog ignored her. "You're such a dumb pet!"

"They know when you call them stupid," Aamir said.

"I doubt he does."

Aamir squatted down, giving the dog a good rub of his velvety chin. He liked dogs. He'd always wanted to own one, and perhaps one day he would – when he was able to look after it, and himself.

"You're an old boy, aren't you? Yes, I know, you like that, don't you?" he murmured, scratching the dog's chin.

Mahnoor gave him one of her hardcore stares, and Aamir felt his cheeks flush. He didn't make a habit of baby-talking with dogs, least of all in front of people like Mahnoor.

"So," she said, "what's going on?"

"Not much."

"What have you been up to?"

"Been to the museum."

"And you decided to stop by … because?"

OK, Mahnoor's tone had definitely slid into an unhappy place. She planted one hand on her hip.

"I've lost something important, and I think it might be here."

"What have you lost now – your manners?"

"My money."

"I haven't seen a wallet lying around anywhere."

"Mind if I take a look?"

Mahnoor did her Bhangra shoulder shrug. She minded for sure, but reluctantly granted him entry. Doughnut was in no rush to slip his head off Aamir's feet, but after a gentle pat on the back, the dog rose. He trotted tightly behind Aamir, following him into the house as if he belonged to him.

"He likes you," Mahnoor observed, not bothering to disguise the surprise in her voice.

"He's clever."

She scoffed. "Right, and how do you know that?"

"His eyes."

"*Pff.*"

Yup, her welcoming mood had done its own disappearing act. It was like there was something left unsaid between them. There was always something left unsaid, like Aamir should have apologized for running away. He hadn't done it on purpose, the ghosting bit. Claire used to complain about him being unreliable, not showing up when he was supposed to, never letting her know what he was doing, unable to commit to any plans. "You're an irresponsible, pathetic, self-centred idiot!" Claire had hissed at Aamir after he forgot about their one-year anniversary. That was six weeks after his Pakistan–India trip, when Aamir had slipped into a drunken depression.

Aamir was still caught up in this shadowy darkness now; he couldn't see the light. And he longed to find his way out of that gloomy place. Normality, stability, peace – that's what he needed. Maybe one day he'd get there. Maybe one day he'd find his way back.

He watched Mahnoor, marching ahead of him, and recalled their conversation about souls and homes. Aamir wasn't the type of person who gave his soul much thought these days. For months he had neglected his body, his life, the people in it, everything. But then there was this moment when Bilal had told him he was going to be a father, and Aamir an uncle. He had felt a jolt in his chest then, a wary sense of excitement, a feeling that life could still be good. It was the first time in months his soul felt soothed.

Aamir had tried to numb it, this form of consciousness that resided within him. He had forgotten what it meant to be truly alive; to breathe in a mouthful of air and feel it fill up his lungs; to bite into a slice of warm toast and savour its crunchy texture; to look at a person and see their kindness.

Mahnoor.

She was a good person. She had invited him home, didn't close the door on him when he had plucked up the courage and decided to return and look for his money. She could have told him to get lost. There was no reason why she should have granted him entry to her house. He was a stranger and he had bad manners – like vanishing without a trace, or breaking up with his girlfriend via text, or bringing shame to his family.

But he needed to eat, and he needed money to do so. When he had trudged up the hill to find Mahnoor's house, he wasn't sure whether he would be brave enough to ring the bell. He had lingered outside the front door for a few minutes, weighing his options. But then she'd suddenly opened the door, the dog by her side, and here he was, shuffling behind her like a kid in trouble.

Now that he knew about her sadness – the dead cousin Mai had mentioned – he could see it. Her steps were heavy; her head hung low; her arms dangled by her side as if they didn't belong there.

Mahnoor glanced at him as they entered the conservatory. Aamir spotted her dad weeding in the garden. The father took no notice of him or Mahnoor, who lifted a couple of cushions off the settee to search for the money. The dog stayed by Aamir's feet, glued to his side. Aamir could have sworn the beagle had watery eyes. Someone should take him to the vet – surely there was a remedy for that.

"Nothing. I can't see anything," Mahnoor said, scanning the airy room. "You must have lost your wallet somewhere else."

"It's not a wallet; it's cash."

"How much, like a bundle?"

Aamir could tell her the truth, but he wasn't about to lose his common sense. That would make him look poor and pathetic, which he was.

"Fifty pounds," he lied.

"How do you lose fifty pounds?"

Aamir said nothing, feeling a tinge of guilt. He hated lying. It was one of the things his father had preached about all the time. "Your tongue becomes poisoned when you lie," he used to tell Aamir, adding a stony glare that was supposed to instil fear in him. And Aamir had a poisonous tongue, like that of a snake.

He shuddered. He had to stay focused. Aamir's eyes wandered around the room. Yesterday he had sat in that weird round chair over there, that papasan thing. He only knew the name of it because Claire had owned one.

He took a couple of steps forward, squinting. There was something small, purple and papery stuck in a crease of the grey fabric. His heart skipped. Yes! He tugged the note free and gripped the money in his hand, feeling a wave of relief wash over him. He could finally buy food. He would be OK now; he could get back to Cardiff if he had to, and life would sort itself out. Somehow. He hoped.

"Oh, you've found it," Mahnoor said. "I thought fifty-pound notes are red?"

Aamir stuffed the money into his pocket, red-faced, his agile hands moving fast. Mahnoor had seen the twenty-pound note. Never mind. He had fulfilled his mission and it was time to go. Baked beans. He would buy himself a tin of them and munch them in a sandwich. Bread and beans, that would keep him going. Maa would be appalled at his choice of food.

"You have got to be kidding me!" someone exclaimed, and he whirled around to look at her.

Not again. Mai, the friend who hated him.

"Why are you *here*?" she asked incredulously.

"Aamir," Mahnoor said calmly, "is joining us for lunch."

21
noori

"So how are you guys related?" Dad asked, sitting at the dining table and stuffing a heap of spicy potatoes into his mouth.

Mai started coughing. All eyes were on her, except Aamir's. He had retreated into a world of his own; flown to some celestial place. Food heaven. The moment he had slouched down next to Noori, his body relaxed.

Noori had not seen him at peace before. The frown, the tight lips, the stiff shoulders – they all disappeared within an instant. When Mum served him first, placing a full plate of vegetables, lentils, rice and various dips, samosas and rotis in front of him, the mask dropped. She saw the real Aamir, and the real Aamir clearly hadn't had a proper meal in ages. When he thanked Mum, Noori heard his gratitude. And when he took his first bite of the roti, nibbling the flatbread, his eyes closed, savouring the moment.

He had lied about the money. She had seen the twenty-pound note that he slipped into his pocket. Clearly he would not have made the embarrassing choice of returning to Noori and her family if he wasn't in desperate need of cash and help. That was when Noori decided to offer him lunch.

She couldn't send him away – being homeless wasn't a joke. It was a serious matter that most people didn't take seriously. It was easy to ignore other people's problems, but other people's problems would, in some kind of roundabout way, often become your own.

Noori stared at her dad, quenching the need to expose his lies. He had plenty of problems, and he was vocal about them. His biggest concern? Brexit, and all the mayhem that followed. Every day he'd go on about it, and she was fed up with hearing him quote stupid politicians, as if that would change anything. "This country is doomed," he mumbled to himself all the time, giving his kids a wistful stare.

Noori watched her dad chew on a potato. *He* was the one who should be interrogated, not Mai. Noori couldn't forgive him. His hypocrisy made her furious. If the rest of the family knew what Noori knew, they would be appalled. And she couldn't keep his act of treason to herself forever. She had to let it all out. Soon.

"What did you say?" Dad asked, still staring at Mai and expecting an answer to his question.

"I didn't say anything; I was coughing," Mai said.

"It doesn't matter how Mai is related to Aamir," Noori said. "They're cousins, full stop."

"Not real cousins; he was adopted," Mai said, scratching her neck. "That's right. Someone in my family adopted him, so there are no blood ties between us, no attachments, nothing."

"That's a bit harsh, dear," Mum said, throwing Mai a concerned look.

Mai shrugged. "Well, life is harsh. I didn't even know about Aamir's existence until I met him this week, so there we go."

"How strange," Dad said, frowning at Mai's cousin.

Mum, on the other hand, offered Aamir a friendly smile. Noori's mum had been watching him in quiet fascination, waiting for the right moment to address him.

"Aamir," Mum said. "I have to say you remind me of my great-uncle in Pakistan; you have the same eyes. He too was an adoptee, in a way. They found him, a little boy, all alone. His parents had lost him in the partition of India; it was—"

"Mum, you've told that story a thousand times," Noori said.

Noori hated that story. It was so sad. The little boy who had become separated from his parents when they fled their home in Lahore in 1947. The little boy who grew up and kept looking for his lost parents, never finding them. It broke Noori's heart. His name was Inayat.

"Noori's right," Mum said to Aamir. "No need to bring this up now. We should talk about more joyful things. So how long are you staying in Bristol, Aamir?"

Mum was beaming then, knowing Aamir enjoyed her food. The only way to compliment her was by letting her know she was a fabulous cook.

Aamir cleared his throat. Noori wasn't sure if he had even followed the conversation. He had been too fixated on his food, devouring it in slow motion.

"I'm leaving today," Aamir said, sounding doubtful.

"Oh, of course, silly question." Mum turned her head to revert her attention back to Mai. "You and your parents are off to France tonight. How could I forget, when Doughnut is going to be our special guest for the next two weeks?"

Doughnut let out a sniff. He was lying under the table; Noori could see his head poking out. He had settled on Aamir's feet again and looked pleased to have found a new favourite cushion.

"Yes, my cousin … he's leaving right after lunch," Mai said. "And we'll probably never see each other again because he lives really far away."

"How far is far?" Mum asked. She was so nosy all the time.

"Somewhere, up in…" Mai faltered. "Up in Scotland."

"Ah, so you're related through your dad."

"Yeah, but my father doesn't like to bring it up."

"Why not?"

"It wasn't exactly a legal adoption."

The twins, who up until this point had not uttered a word, gawked at Aamir. Everybody did, except for Noori, who eyeballed Mai for being such a stupid liar. Noori should not have put her faith in Mai. She watched too many legal dramas.

"This is quite some story," Dad noted. "Sounds like something out of a movie."

"A bad movie," Noori said, kicking Mai's leg under the table.

"Well, I'm not the one who—" Mai stopped herself in the middle of the sentence. They all waited expectantly for her to finish, except for Noori, who prayed she wouldn't.

Noori made a valiant effort to change the subject. "All right, let's discuss other, more important matters," she said.

"There are indeed plenty of things that are worth discussing," Dad agreed. He glanced at Noori's headscarf. She was still wearing the pink one. Noori was intrigued by the fact that nobody had mentioned it again. It was like they were all afraid of her.

"You know what I read in the paper today?" Dad asked, filling the silence.

Nobody was looking at him. The twins were still analysing Aamir, no doubt trying to figure out the dodgy dealings behind his supposed adoption. Mum was refilling her glass of lemon water. Mai was probably weighing up Noori's novelty earring collection in her head, knowing she deserved at least one pair after agreeing to go along with Noori's ridiculous idea. Aamir was stroking Doughnut. And Noori kept her head low, trying not to look at Aamir. He was so quiet.

"You know what people are saying about the last prime minister?" Dad said, somewhat half-heartedly, realizing nobody was paying him much attention.

"I don't care what they say; there's so much else going on in the world," Noori said. "I'm sick of hearing about deceitful politicians."

"I would think we all are," he said, "but they found out—"

"That people are all bloody liars and we should not put our trust in anyone!"

"No need to raise your voice," Dad said, taken aback by her sudden hostility.

"I'm not raising my voice; I'm raising my words."

Aamir stopped patting Doughnut, tilting his head in Noori's direction. Maybe he realized she had just quoted Rumi. Out of all the people present in the room, he was the only one who might have recognized the reference.

"Noori," Mum said warningly. "Let's just enjoy lunch in peace."

"All right." Noori squashed a chickpea with her fork. "We could talk about other stories."

"What stories?" Mum was frowning now, like Dad.

"Like the story Dad used to tell us, about Pinocchio and what happens when we lie."

Noori had believed her father as a kid, thinking her nose would grow if she told a porky pie. She'd worried she'd end up with a big beak, and she had, but it turned out that had nothing to do with her lies. She had been so naive.

Her parents were observing her, watching on, waiting for Noori to explain herself.

"What's your point?" Dad asked, all innocent.

"You've lied, that's my point," Noori said, still raising her words. "About me."

Dad was shifting in his chair, his cheeks turning rosy. Everyone else was staring at the quarrelling father–daughter duo. Didn't he know what she was referring to? The phone call, late at night, last week, when he thought everyone was fast asleep?

Noori glanced at Aamir, the boy who had entered her world out of the blue. He looked uneasy, so out of place in this sudden family quarrel when all he clearly wanted was a good meal.

"Why are you so quiet?" Noori asked into the silence. "Feeling uncomfortable, Dad?"

"Since when do you care about other people's feelings?" he retorted, no longer treating Noori like the fragile daughter. Finally he was ready to battle this one out. "You're so wrapped up in your own world, you don't want to know about anyone else's."

"You're right," Noori said. "I don't care about liars and their poisonous tongues."

Mum banged her fork down on her empty plate. "Enough drama," she said. "I'm going to make chai now. Who wants some?" She was good at ignoring Noori's outbursts, and knew the only way to appease her daughter was by serving her favourite drink. Noori didn't want to fall for the chai trap again, but she couldn't help herself.

"Me," Noori said, sighing with resignation.

"How about you, Aamir?" Mum asked in her motherly voice.

"Yes," he said. "Please."

The way Aamir said *please* made Noori feel something. Her fumes of anger fizzled. A sudden wave of embarrassment washed over her, and something *else* as well. Munazzah would have known what it was. She would have come up with a smart, non-precocious line, summing up Noori's weird emotions in one sentence. But this feeling, it was something Noori hadn't felt before.

And it bugged her.

22
aamir

Aamir threw Mahnoor a furtive glance as they marched to the front door. He had thanked her parents profusely before getting up so damn quickly he'd nearly taken half the table with him. It was high time to leave, which was totally fine. Aamir was good at goodbyes. He could pack a forty-litre backpack and leave his entire life behind, pretending it had never happened. Maa, Pa, Claire – they were all a thing of the past now.

That pain in his chest, though. It was real, almost as if he was going to have a heart attack.

Maa had broken his heart.

Pa had disregarded his heart.

Bilal never knew about it.

And Claire had toyed with it.

He'd done her wrong. And then she had flipped out, turning up on his doorstep that day, lying to Pa about Aamir.

"Your son," Claire had said, "is a bastard child."

Claire was a stranger to Pa, appearing out of the blue calling him names. His son, his Aamir, the youngest of his two children, was not a bastard. He had not been born out of wedlock. Claire had sneered, laughed in his face.

"You know what your son gets up to when you're not around? What he did to me?" she had said.

And then the drunken bathroom scene happened and Pa had kicked Aamir out. What were they doing now he was gone? Did they have regrets, like he did, or were they too proud, too set in their ways, to think of themselves as culpable in Aamir's fall from grace?

He couldn't undo what had happened between him and Pa and Claire. Before he had vanished into thin air and his phone had been stolen, he had received two calls from her. He didn't answer – he wasn't stupid. Claire had lied to Pa – in part, at least. She could have saved him a lot of trouble if she'd kept her mouth shut that day. The day he was kicked out.

Aamir could forgive a lot, but not everything. That one lie, the one story she had made up, knowing it would make Aamir's life a lot more complicated – he couldn't let her off that one. And the worst bit was that Pa had believed her.

"He gets drunk; he takes drugs; he's a regular with the girls," Claire had told Pa while Aamir was puking his guts out, unaware how shocked his father must have been to hear those words. Pa knew next to nothing about Aamir's double life. "I'm just one of the girls your son used, and when he got me pregnant, he made me abort the baby."

The baby story was a lie. And Aamir had only cheated on

Claire once, and that was after he had broken up with her last month – but at this point she still considered him to be her boyfriend. So in reality he didn't cheat at all. And the girl Aamir had hooked up with: he'd forgotten her face but remembered her name (Rhian). He'd recently snogged her at a party and that was it. They had both been wasted. But Claire had heard about it, felt betrayed, and sought revenge.

"You're not my son," Pa had said, barging into the bathroom and recounting the whole Claire story to him in disgust when Aamir was nursing a hangover, crouched on the floor after enduring another violent bout of puking. Aamir had made his father believe he was ill, and Pa had believed him. Until Claire had shown up and filled him in on Aamir's other life. It was then his father realized what was really going on, making his disappointment known.

Pa was strict and he was upset, but he could forgive and forget. He had lectured Aamir about women and alcohol, preached about sins and so on. But the fake abortion story had got under his skin. He could not forgive Aamir for what he had done to the girl. Pa knew Claire wasn't one hundred per cent innocent, but he blamed Aamir for getting involved with her in the first place – a girl without religion.

As someone who based his entire existence on his faith, secular people worried Pa. And he had assumed his son to be a believer until Aamir slurred those words about God. He shouldn't have insulted Pa's God. That was the moment their fragile bond broke completely.

Fathers and sons. Fathers and daughters. Aamir wasn't

the only one who had parental issues. Mahnoor's family had seemed normal in a malfunctioning way, but it was clear there was so much else going on beneath the surface, which was why he wanted to leave as quickly as possible. In a way he would have liked to stay for some nice family chat – he could deal with a bit of bickering – and a home was a home, even if it wasn't Aamir's home. But there was enough drama in his life.

Mahnoor had offered to walk him to the door, jumping at the chance to leave. The two had reached the hallway now, and Aamir was staring at the big black door and Mahnoor's big black eyes.

Yes, this definitely had to be their final goodbye.

23
noori

Toothpaste. On his black shirt.

Noori couldn't stop glaring at the white fleck on his top. She wanted to spit into her hand and scour the spot off. But that would have been weird and slightly disgusting, even she knew that.

"You've got some stuff on your shirt," Noori said, pointing to her cleavage until she realized she was pointing to her cleavage and encouraging Aamir to gawk at it too. He didn't.

"Toothpaste," she said. "Right there."

She went for it anyway. Her thumb was on his chest, and she felt the cotton rubbing against her skin as she wiped the gritty bits of toothpaste off.

Noori retracted her hand when she belatedly comprehended how odd it was for her to fondle Aamir's chest. If he had done the same to her, she would have slapped him hard. But his usual poker face remained; he didn't seem to mind.

"Got any plans for this afternoon?" Noori blurted, trying to get the image of Aamir rubbing her chest out of her messy head.

"Nope."

"So where you off to?"

"The harbourside."

Noori waited for him to elaborate, but Aamir wasn't the sort of person to elaborate. She had worked that out early on.

"What's in your backpack?" she asked, out of the blue and out of context.

"My life."

Noori glanced him up and down. "You're smarter than you look."

He smiled, vaguely.

How bizarre. Aamir had said he wanted to leave, couldn't escape fast enough after guzzling down his chai, yet now he was loitering, shifting his weight from one leg to the other like he wasn't in a hurry to scoot off. Where would life take him? It was none of her business, but Noori's entrepreneurial spirit called to her. She wanted to take on this business although her risk management team, consisting of three bickering versions of herself, advised against it.

"You're also smarter than you look," Aamir said.

"I'm extremely smart," Noori said. "Although my year two PE teacher wouldn't agree. She used to say I was too thick to catch a ball."

"She sounds like someone who should raise her words." Aamir paused, now leaning leisurely against the front door, frowning. "But not everyone gets Rumi."

Noori felt her pupils dilate. According to her biology tutor, that happens when we see something that stimulates the brain. Aamir had stirred something up in there and that something lay in the dense air, crackling. He was so unusual. And Noori liked unusual.

"So why are you into Rumi?" Noori asked. "He's become this cult figure, hasn't he? Like people know about him even if they don't get him."

"Yeah, but that's because he speaks the truth, and people need to hear the truth, today, more so than ever."

Noori looked doubtful. "I don't know. I feel like people want to believe in fake lies and ignore the truth; just look at what happened..."

No. Not now, Noori. Mum's right. Don't ruin the moment.

"I know what you mean," he said.

"You do?"

"Sure."

Noori frowned. "What are we talking about?"

"The same thing," Aamir said. He shrugged. She had come to like that particular shrug. "The state of the world."

Indeed.

And what a weird world Noori was inhabiting in that moment. Had he read her mind? No, of course not. But this dude was a thinker, and Noori was a thinker too. And right then, she was thinking about Aamir.

He didn't reveal much about himself, turning himself into this walking mystery, a Rubik's cube that Noori, for no explicable reason, was trying to assemble. He was hiding stuff;

he didn't want his fellow human beings to see what he was made of. But deep down, in every grotto, there was a treasure trove. And that was where Aamir was keeping his true emotions.

Wow. Was that what Munazzah had meant when she talked about people's flaws being a treasure trove? And how had that ingenious thought just popped into her head? Noori couldn't help but be impressed with herself.

"What are you smiling about?" Aamir asked.

"My smart arse," Noori said. "Take that, Mrs Hounslow!"

"Who's that?"

"My former PE teacher. She used to give me night terrors."

"I had a teacher like that."

"Really?"

"Yeah, Mr Bush. He told me to become a bus driver, like my dad."

"There's nothing wrong with being a bus driver."

"I know."

Aamir fell back into silence. Why was he like that? He said stuff, and then just stopped. It was confusing because Noori enjoyed listening to him. His voice was nice, she mused, well suited for the type of podcast where people discuss art history and the like, topics that are meant to bore you, but you can't switch off because the presenter's soothing voice delivers a top-notch audio massage.

"Thanks, by the way," Aamir said, rubbing the back of his neck.

"What for?"

"Lunch. It was delicious."

"I know. My mum's the best cook."

"Mums always are."

"Nah, you should see some of the stuff Mai's mother serves up. She's into frog legs."

"They taste like chicken."

"You've tried some?"

"Sure."

"*Chee, chee!* How gross."

Aamir half smiled, but he wasn't looking at Noori. He was gazing past her at a spot on the wall, as if someone friendly was standing there, a ghost, or something freaky like that.

"What are you looking at?" she asked.

"Nothing."

"But it looks like you're looking at something. Or someone."

Aamir's gaze drifted from the wall to Noori's expectant face. The smile was gone. He was all serious again, and Noori expected him now to stroll through the open front door that was allowing a welcome cool breeze to flood through the house. But Aamir stood still, showing no intention of running out of Noori's life just yet.

"You," he said, clearing his throat. "You remind me of someone, that's all."

"Like who?"

"My maa."

24
aamir

What the hell was wrong with him?

He had mentioned both his parents in front of her. Aamir didn't want to bring them up – he'd tried to bury them deep in the back of his mind, where the two took up little space. His parents were shadows that followed him around, and Aamir wasn't afraid of shadows. Sure, he couldn't outrun a shadow, but given the right light and weather conditions, he could make them vanish.

Aamir had felt caged in his entire life and now he was liberated, for a while at least, roaming the streets of Bristol on his own, doing whatever the heck he wanted. He could sleep under the sky. He could sit on a bench for hours. He could brush his teeth in a museum.

The toothpaste. That had been odd. Mahnoor had rubbed that speck of toothpaste off his shirt very vigorously. He had felt confused, hoping she'd stop, and then she had, and he'd spotted the embarrassment in her eyes.

She was just … weird. But the truth was, Aamir was finding out he liked weird. It's not like he could claim to be normal. Normal people don't get kicked out of their homes. And most of all, they don't pretend to be someone's illegally adopted cousin and have lunch with a bunch of strangers.

"I remind you of your mother – like I'm old?" Mahnoor said, sounding perplexed.

"No," he protested. "That's not what I meant."

"You need to learn to communicate properly if you want to avoid misunderstandings!"

This was what always happened when Aamir shared personal info. People didn't get him; they misconstrued him. And then he would feel the need to justify himself, when he was done with explaining. But Mahnoor was glaring at him, expecting an explanation. So he gave her one.

"It's what you said." Aamir swallowed. His mouth had run out of spit. "My mother used to say that."

"Say what?"

"*Chee, chee.*"

Mahnoor gave him a puzzling look. He felt like he was under interrogation; he knew she'd follow up on the information he had just provided. Her mind was sharp; she picked up on little details. The toothpaste. The twenty pounds. His backpack. His life. He braced himself against the need to run away.

"Your mum *used to* say *chee*," Mahnoor said, ruminating and rubbing her spotty cheeks. "Doesn't she say it any more?"

"No." Pause. "She died," Aamir said, the words fizzing out of his mouth.

His tongue was numb. And something changed right then, between them. It was like the Rubik's cube finally clicked into place. The way she gazed at him with acute awareness, like she knew where he was coming from. It was a level of understanding he hadn't experienced before, and it all happened in silence, in a space of stillness.

"Death and stuff," Mahnoor said after a while, "it sucks."

"Yeah, it sucks you in."

"Until you dissolve."

"Until you're nothing."

Aamir nodded. It looked like he and Mahnoor grieved in the same way.

"It feels like being lost, doesn't it?" she asked softly.

"Yup." He swallowed hard.

"Aamir," Mahnoor said, her voice low. "I think I know why you're really carrying that backpack all the time."

Of course she knew. That girl was smart.

25
noori

The words echoed through her fuzzy head. Aamir's maa was dead. That was bad, like really bad. Noori couldn't even begin to imagine a life without her mother. She had a sudden longing to run to the kitchen and give her mum a huge hug just to show her appreciation that she, Dr Gurjar-Oates, was still amongst the living.

"It's not something to be embarrassed about," Noori said.

"I'm not."

"So do you need a place to stay, like for a couple of nights?"

"Huh?" He rubbed his chin, looking almost embarrassed – for her.

OK, this was plain nuts. She had no authority to say those things or make any such decisions, but what was she supposed to do? Noori was human, and humans want to help, at least the decent ones do, and she considered herself to be an exquisitely decent human being.

Aamir raised one eyebrow, then another, and she spotted a long scar running down the side of his forehead. How had she not noticed that earlier?

"I was saying," Noori said, faster than she intended in case she changed her mind. "Next door, our neighbours, Mai's place, you know, they're off on holiday this evening, and we're supposed to look after the house, so you could look after it, in a way, for a few days or so, until, you know, uh, you know what you're gonna do? I dunno. Was just thinking. The spare key, it's in the bird box, front garden…"

This was mental! Noori was mental – words were just spilling out and there was no way that she could take them back. Mai was right. Maybe Noori was suffering from grief-induced madness. But now she had offered her help, her deed was done, and it was up to Aamir to take up her offer. Or not. She hoped he would turn her down.

Please turn it down, she thought.

Instant regret kicked in. She had just offered up *someone else's house*. Mai would hate her, and Mai's parents would be appalled if they ever found out what she had just suggested.

There was only so much Noori was able to get away with. Yes, Munazzah's death had messed her up, and people showed understanding to a certain extent. But Noori knew she had crossed a boundary here. People got shot for crossing boundaries – if you entered hostile territory.

Aamir gawked at her, the prickly stubble on his chin

standing on end. Noori had never felt so dumb in her life. Her PE teacher was right. Noori was as thick as a brick. And she still couldn't catch a ball.

"I don't need a place to stay," Aamir said, scratching his neck again.

Was he nervous?

"I'm on my way to the harbourside because my brother lives there."

"The harbourside." Now it was Noori's turn to scratch the back of her sweaty neck. "Heard it's haunted. The SS *Great Britain*, that is. The ghost of the captain's supposed to live on the ship."

"I don't believe in ghosts."

"I was joking."

He smirked; she didn't.

What were they doing? They were prolonging this scene unnecessarily. And Noori still felt stupid.

"Well, I should go back inside," Noori said, pointing vaguely behind her. She could hear her parents in the kitchen, loading the dishwasher. The twins would have retreated to their rooms. And Mai? She'd be munching leftover samosas. This guy had been offering nothing but distractions; there were far more important things happening in her life. Noori didn't have much time left with Mai. She wouldn't see her for months, and in a strange way she was dreading saying goodbye to her today. Not that she expected Mai to die on her trip to France, but who knew? Ever since Munazzah's passing, she'd been expecting the unexpected.

But all these thoughts aside, she was moving to Pakistan in four days' time and she had barely thought about it ever since bumping into this Mister Kapoor lookalike. It was time to get her priorities straight again.

Noori held out her arm, businesslike. Aamir glanced at it and then they both held hands briefly. It felt weird and hot and sticky, and Noori was glad when it was over.

"Have a nice life," Noori said, trying to sound polite and not sad.

"Yeah, you too."

He nodded and shuffled down the path to the creaking gate.

Aamir cut a sad figure, Noori thought as she closed the door. Maybe she should have asked him for his email address so they could keep in touch.

Doughnut whined behind her. Like Noori, he glanced wistfully at the door.

26
aamir

He had planned to ask Mahnoor for her number, but then she had almost shoved him out of the door, like she wanted to get rid of him. Anyway. What would have been the point? It was not like they were going to become friends. He had to sort out his crap.

Again Aamir found himself staring at the skeleton of the SS *Great Britain*, but this time remembering Mahnoor's words about the captain and his ghost. A slow shiver ran down his spine. He didn't believe in ghosts, but Maa had, often recounting chilling stories of djinns, evil spirits, and claiming to have seen her dead grandfather's shadow in her childhood home. Passing that ship for the umpteenth time gave him a funny feeling in the pit of his stomach.

When he eventually arrived at Bilal's flat, Aamir realized his prayers had been answered. There was his brother's flashy car. Bilal was home. At last.

The seagulls' scornful cackling echoed in his ears as he rang the bell and the entrance door opened, as if by magic. Aamir trundled up the flight of stairs. They lived on the first floor, Bilal and Umaira, and he felt his cheeks glow as he set eyes on his brother's confused face as he waited in the doorway, a cup of coffee in one hand. This was certainly a surprise, his eyebrows seemed to say.

Bilal spoke first. "Aamir? What are you doing here? Abbu said you weren't home. And why have you had your phone switched off? I've been trying to call you non-stop, man."

"Had my phone nicked," Aamir said, thinking what an inappropriate way that was to start a conversation with his brother after not having seen him in weeks.

Bilal looked different. His shirt was creased, and he hadn't shaved in days. That look of anguish. Was he stressed? Did Bilal know what had happened between Aamir and Pa? His brother seemed clueless when he asked – no, told – Aamir to come in, more or less shoving him into this nice apartment that they were going to give up once the baby was there and they had found a more family suitable property, or so Bilal had said in the past.

There was no sound; not even the fridge made a gurgling noise as Bilal ushered Aamir into the kitchen, swigging down the rest of his coffee. He was in a rush, that much was clear. Aamir wondered where Umaira was.

"Where's the missus?" he asked, watching his brother open the fridge.

"What do you mean, where's the missus?" Bilal barked.

"Where've you been these past three days? She's in hospital, that's where. Has Abbu not told you?"

Abbu. Pa. Aamir had obviously missed something. Something big.

"I haven't heard a thing. I haven't been home since Friday," Aamir now said, feeling like he was talking to the younger version of his father.

"Where've you been?" Bilal asked, narrowing his eyes.

"Has Pa not told you?"

"Obviously not," Bilal snapped, giving his brother an irritated scowl. "Just like he failed to inform you about Umaira's pregnancy complications."

"Is she OK?"

"She needs bed rest. They're keeping her in the hospital; she's been bleeding for days."

"I'm s-sorry," Aamir stuttered. He swallowed, finally making sense of his brother's tense reaction, the anxiety in his voice, his preoccupation. That was why his brother was so irritated by the fact Aamir had shown up without invitation. It was an inconvenient time to barge into his life. Bilal had other, more important things on his mind and it was selfish of Aamir to be here now, asking him for a big favour when Umaira was unwell, when someone else's plight mattered far more than his.

"She'll be OK; they both will be OK, inshallah," Bilal said, heaving out a big sigh. "But I need to get back. I just came home to shower."

"That sounds, um, intense," Aamir mumbled, having no clue what his sister-in-law was going through. If only Maa were here, he thought. She'd make it all OK.

"Yes, well. Abbu's on the way. I asked him not to come, but he's worried," Bilal said, finally plopping onto a chair, his weight making it creak.

"Wait," Aamir said, feeling a strange and excruciating pain in his chest, as if someone were stabbing him in the heart. "Pa's on the way, like, right now?"

Bilal ignored his question. "Look, what's going on?"

"So Pa really hasn't said anything to you about the fact he's kicked me out?"

Bilal fluttered his eyelids, as if he needed a moment to comprehend this new information. He licked his lips – they looked dehydrated, Aamir noted – and then rose to his feet again and ambled to the window overlooking the harbour. He was silent for the longest time.

Aamir was beginning to feel a growing sense of dread. Pa was on the way. He could arrive any minute. He couldn't face him now. But what had Aamir been thinking? That he'd never see or speak to his father again?

It was just that he thought he would have more time. To process. To think. To plan.

"What have you done this time?" Bilal asked, his voice strained, his face still turned away. "You know what? I'd prefer not to know. But Abbu must have had a good reason for losing his temper."

Aamir stayed silent. He had expected this reaction. Still, he had hoped for a tiny bit of brotherly loyalty. He should have known that coming here would mean more trouble, not less.

Maa would be ashamed, he thought. She would never have let things come this far.

"I haven't done anything bad." Aamir could hear how he sounded. Like a petulant child.

"I know about your partying, Aamir. I'm not stupid," Bilal said, swinging his head round, his arms crossed, his eyes piercing through Aamir's. "Was it drugs, or did you get involved with some dodgy people? You haven't done anything illegal, have you?"

"You're…" Though Aamir couldn't quite believe the last question, he stopped himself. He wasn't going to aggravate the situation; he would have to swallow his dignity. "No, I've not done anything illegal. There was a girl, Claire, and Pa wasn't happy about—"

"I see," Bilal said, letting out a moan. "All of this because of a girl? Really?"

"As if you never had girlfriends before you met Umaira."

"That's not the point," Bilal said, unfazed by Aamir's comment. "You've been acting mental for months. We're all missing Maa, but we're not losing our minds over her loss. You need to grow up, Aamir. Stop being such a—"

And here Bilal used an Urdu word that was both offensive and profane. Pa would not have been amused, and neither was Aamir. His brother had not been there when Maa died; he didn't see it happen, didn't blame himself, didn't spend hours each day wondering whether he could have done anything to prevent her death. Bilal had no idea what Aamir had gone through, knew nothing of his torment. And Aamir didn't even have anyone to share his painful thoughts with. Nobody understood. Pa and Bilal and Aamir may have all been riding the same wave, but each of them sat in a different boat. His was a ghost ship.

So much for his brother coming to his aid. It had all been wishful thinking on Aamir's part that Bilal might even attempt to comprehend where Aamir was coming from. Aamir was not without blame, but he had come here and swallowed his ego only to be treated like Bilal's dumb little brother who did dumb little things all the time.

He had two choices: to stay and listen to Bilal's constant reproaches. Or not stay. It was that simple, and yet at the same time it was the most complex problem he had ever faced in his seventeen years. To make matters worse, the doorbell rang and Bilal darted out of the kitchen only to reappear moments later with Pa by his side.

Aamir's heart sank. It stung so badly, seeing *him*. Why did Pa have to show up now, at this exact moment in time, and remind Aamir what a lousy son he was? His first instinct was to run. His second was to apologize.

Aamir did not expect to see his father looking so old and worn. It was as though he had aged by decades in the three days Aamir had been gone. "You're not my son," Pa had said, and still here they were, father and son, staring at each other without uttering a single word. Aamir could read Pa's mind: shame.

"Aamir," Pa said, his voice breaking. "Why are you here?"

Aamir feigned nonchalance. "No worries, I was just on my way out," he said. "I'll come back another time, Bilal."

And that was that. He didn't listen to Bilal's calls to wait, wait, *wait*. For a moment he hesitated, felt his knees go weak, his heart go soft. He almost changed his mind then. What if he stayed? What if he listened to what they had to say even if he didn't want to? Maybe they'd try and help him, if he let them, if he didn't continue to shut them out. They were the only family he had left, after all. Even if they didn't show it in conventional ways, they all still cared for one another. But he kept walking, marching himself out of that building, his legs carrying him back to the ghost ship, right where he belonged.

DAY 4

27
noori

"Stop it!" Noori roared early in the morning as the birds were chirping in the trees and the sun was rising, like Doughnut, who had placed himself on top of Noori's bare feet, slobbering all over her toes, licking her nails with gusto.

Noori shivered, but it wasn't the haunting notion of paranormal spirits that made her hide under her soft duvet. She cringed at the thought of having offered Aamir a place to stay at Mai's.

A heavy paw on Noori's shin stopped her thinking process. Doughnut wriggled around, his head emerging from under the cover. They were eye to eye now. Did the dog know no boundaries?

"Go back to sleep," she mumbled.

Doughnut did his poo face in response. He needed to get out, fast.

"Man, can't you keep it in for, like, two more hours?"

With no other option but to let him out so he could do his gross business, she sluggishly rolled out of bed. It was early so everyone would still be asleep, but she couldn't help but notice that she really did look a state.

Her pyjamas consisted of short shorts and a top with a sparkly unicorn printed across its back. And then there was her hair: full of knots and lumps and last night's popcorn that she had munched while watching a Bollywood film in bed, with Doughnut by her side. Doughnut loved Bollywood. He always rubbed the screen with his paws when his favourite actress made an appearance – she looked a bit like Munazzah. Noori grabbed her headscarf, draping it loosely over her hair. Hopefully it would hide the sin within.

"Let's go," she muttered, and Doughnut trotted along eagerly behind her.

The odd pair sneaked through the house. Noori didn't make a sound, her feet light as a feather, her breath thin as, well, air. Doughnut raced out of the back door and disappeared behind a bush. She adjusted her headscarf, wrapping it round her neck a couple of times, but that made her feel like she was suffocating, so she ended up tying it around her head until she had created a messy yet functional turban.

The dog really was taking his time and Noori was starting to feel silly hanging around in her PJs, holding a plastic bag she'd have to use to scoop up a pile of warm turds which Doughnut treated like a trophy. Where *was* he? After waiting another minute, Noori followed his tracks and peered around the bush. No poop, no beagle. Noori's eyes wandered to Mai's

156

empty house. The windows were closed and the lights were off; there was no sign of human existence.

A bark.

Noori craned her head over the hedge and caught sight of the dog. He'd gone next door into Mai's bloody back garden, where he usually did his business. And now he was wagging his tail in excitement, staring at the terrace door, probably thinking Mai was home and would let him in.

Noori called and whistled, but he didn't move. She sighed. Why on earth did she agree to be his temporary carer? Now she had to go into Mai's house to access the back garden and convince him to come back into her house: all before *six in the morning*!

Cranky, sleepy and hungry, Noori made her way next door. The iron gate creaked as she shoved it open, entering the small front garden which was made up of fuchsias in all colours. Noori headed straight for the tree with its twisted branches, finding the little bird box where it was supposed to be. The key should be inside.

It was more than thoughtless, reckless even, to leave a house key outside one's house, but both Mai and her mum regularly forgot their keys. Noori had lost count of the times that she or one of her family had to let their neighbours back into their own home. She cast a hasty glance over her shoulder, making sure no one was watching as she flipped open the roof of the bird box.

Noori's damp fingers fumbled around until she touched something cold that was made of metal. The key. It was still there; of course it was. Lifting it out, she marched towards the front door, slipped it into the lock, and moments later she was reunited with Doughnut, who raced past her, his clumsy old legs scrabbling on the carpet. He had picked up a scent and followed it to the kitchen. Everything was tidy and organized in here. Noori checked the fridge – she was starving – but it was empty, save for a stick of butter.

Doughnut picked up another scent and without warning bolted up the stairs, forcing Noori to chase after him. She discovered the dog outside Mai's bathroom, staring expectantly at the closed door.

"Listen," Noori said. "Mai isn't here."

Doughnut panted and nodded.

"Fine. I'll prove it to you."

Without thinking about it, Noori banged the door open, expecting the place to be a mess because Mai's bathroom was always a mess. And sure enough, clothes and towels were strewn across the tiled floor. Sheesh, she'd even left litres of soapy water in her bathtub.

Disgusting.

Noori scuttled towards the bath and saw a mass of black hair floating in the water. And although Noori was smart, it took her a moment to realize what she was staring at. There was a human body lying submerged in the bathtub. Part of that body – the head, face, shoulders and arms – had dived under the surface, but the rest of it was in plain view.

It was a male body.

"Oh!" Noori shrieked.

Never in her life would she get that picture out of her head.

And a heartbeat later, the head, face, shoulders and arms of that male body emerged, and two horrified eyes gawked back at Noori.

Aamir.

28
aamir

Doughnut flopped into the bathtub making a giant splash. Aamir couldn't believe it. He was mortified. The old dog was frolicking around in the water, his paws scratching Aamir in various tender areas, and Noori was stuck to the spot staring at him. At *him*.

"Oh my – I am so, so sorry," Mahnoor said, blistering with embarrassment. "I didn't see anything, I swear."

They both knew this was a lie. And, if truth be told, there was nothing to be ashamed of.

"I'm not looking; I'm going downstairs now, byeeee," she gabbled, and off she went, slamming the bathroom door behind her.

Doughnut showed no intention of leaving. Aamir wasn't keen on sharing his bath with an animal and slipped out the moment Mahnoor banged the door shut. He had to admit that he had not expected to find himself in this kind of situation.

Aamir hadn't been in the house for long. He had spent another night in the park. After wasting the better part of the twenty quid on a can of lager and two custard slices, he quickly realized this expensive error didn't leave him enough money to buy a train ticket to Cardiff, where he could attempt to stay with one of his mates. So he tried to hitch a ride to his home city, wandering down to where the river flowed under the Clifton Suspension Bridge. There was an A road next to it and Aamir knew it eventually joined the motorway, which headed west to Wales, but no one had stopped and so Aamir was still stuck in fecking Bristol.

He couldn't return to Bilal's place. They didn't want him there, that much was clear. The way Pa had glared at him, the way Bilal had spoken to him, as if he were a naughty child, incapable of being someone worthy of their time. The rising panic had started to return, when he suddenly remembered Mahnoor's proposal. He knew the offer wasn't Mahnoor's to make – in fact it was plain wrong. But right then, what other option did he have?

How could he have known he was going to end up naked in a stranger's bathroom, a crazy, yelping dog by his side and an attractive girl ogling (in a non-perverted sense) his naked body?

At least he was clean. This was the first proper wash he'd had since leaving home. But there was no time to linger, not with Doughnut gaping at his butt. Aamir gathered his clothes, slipped them on, and ambled down the stairs.

There was only one thought going round in his head. Given the fact that the human mind is estimated to think up to eighty thousand thoughts a day, this particular thought was both novel and exceptional: Mahnoor had seen him in the nude. And, judging by her reaction, she wasn't impressed.

29
noori

Noori swung the terrace door open. She needed air. She was flustered, hot and generally horrified. As much as she tried, she couldn't get the image out of her mind – a nude and hairy Aamir, floating in the bathtub, swinging ... low. She'd never be able to look him in the eye again without being reminded of that sizeable moment. For heaven's sake, she shouldn't have been put in this position – he wasn't supposed to be here! But she couldn't ignore the irony. It was her stupid invitation that had put her in this position.

She heard a door bang shut. Had Aamir left again? It wouldn't surprise her. Noori shouldn't care, but deep down she did. It was almost like she was supposed to bump into him at random. Like there was someone up there – aliens, Munazzah, maybe aliens *and* Munazzah – manipulating the universe. A force that was making sure Aamir's and Noori's paths crossed over and over again. Admittedly in very odd ways. But why?

What was the point? She'd be off to Lahore in three days; there was no time to make friends with a stranger.

But man, if Aamir were an actor in a Bollywood movie, he'd play the perfect outcast and she would probably watch that movie ten times in a row because it would never stop intriguing her… OK, now she sounded ridiculous.

"Stupid," she said, muttering to herself.

"Are you talking to me?"

Noori twisted her head in slow motion to find herself gazing at Aamir. He looked different. He was clean and had shaved off his stubble. His damp black hair hung down his angular face. And she could smell the herbal soap sticking to his skin. Patchouli.

"Yes," Noori said, making a point of meeting Aamir's eyes, however tricky it was not to divert her gaze. "I heard the door, thought you'd taken off without saying a word. Again. What are you still doing here anyway? You're supposed to be at your brother's."

"There's been an unexpected change of plan."

"You know what? This is starting to get on my nerves. I can't stand liars."

"I'm not lying," Aamir said with a straight face. "I should have, I mean, I would have…"

"Shoulda, coulda, woulda," Noori mumbled to herself, grunting.

Boy, this guy could get to her like no one else. He weaselled his way in and out of her life and always came up with dumb excuses. She'd rather be told the truth – even if it hurt.

Aamir obviously thought she was thick. He didn't think she could see through him. That bloody patchouli scent, she loved it. Why did he have to smell so nice, causing unnecessary distraction? And his eyes. He looked so vulnerable. But she had to remind herself none of this was OK. If he wanted Noori on his side, he'd have to give her something in return. The truth, and nothing but the effing truth.

Noori cleared her throat, widened her stance, rearranged her turban, placed her hands on her hips and spoke with clear frustration, unable to disguise her annoyance.

"So, what are you saying, or not saying?" she asked. "I always feel like you're not saying something."

"I-I…" he stuttered, struggling to maintain eye contact.

She shook her head. "You know what? I don't care."

"No, hold on," Aamir protested. "The truth is none of this was planned, I promise. It all happened in a moment of madness, really, and now I'm in Bristol I'm glad my plan hasn't exactly worked out, because…"

And here he stopped, swallowing, staring right at her with his tea-stained eyes.

"What?" Noori snapped. "Because you got beaten up by a bunch of thugs?"

"Because I." Aamir took a deep breath. "Because. I. Met. You."

His words sank in. It took Noori a moment to comprehend her emotional turmoil because she was feeling far too many things at once: disbelief (was he telling the truth?), embarrassment (the nude scene), confusion (what did he mean?).

"What do you mean – because you met me?" she asked.

"Would you just explain what you're on about? Why you're here? Why the hell we keep meeting in this way? WHY YOU'RE IN MY LIFE?" She hadn't expected to shout that last question. Aamir looked slightly alarmed. But she was furious. Somehow this boy – in the space of what, three days? – had completely infiltrated her already confused existence. It was – *he* was – too much. "And don't lie to me."

The startled look on his face: it was as if her outburst had caused him to rethink, as if he realized he couldn't mess around with her any more. Noori, they both knew, had shown Aamir an insane amount of kindness, without hesitation. She deserved to hear the truth, even if it was only part of it, and if he couldn't give her an ounce now, he never would.

"All right," he said, heaving out a sigh. "My father kicked me out because he doesn't want a loser as a son, and I can't blame him. I was hoping to stay here in Bristol with my brother for a while, but he doesn't want me. He has enough going on in his life as it is, and I have no money right now, no food, no home. Until I get back to Cardiff, that is, and maybe crash at a mate's place for a few days. That's why I'm still here." He paused, hesitating. "It could be worse."

"Sounds pretty bad to me," Noori said, somewhat calmer. "Your dad kicked you out. Why?"

"He found out about some of the things I did."

"Like?"

"I was messed up." Aamir rubbed his smooth, stubble-free chin. "I wasn't in a good place, hurt people's feelings; it wasn't nice. I made some mistakes."

"I see."

Noori did not see. She wanted more from him. More explanation. She did not want any more cryptic Aamir.

This whole thing almost felt like a play to her, and a pretty convoluted one at that. It needed more direction, but she couldn't do that without food inside her. She was starving.

"I can't do this on an empty stomach," Noori said. "Let's go into the kitchen."

"I'm such a shit magnet," Aamir mumbled to himself, following Noori.

"I wouldn't be here if you were," she said.

Aamir flicked her a grateful nod in response. Odd. Her seeing him naked was all it took for him to suddenly feel at ease. People should get naked more often. He seemed less worried about exposing himself now. She chided herself. She had to stop dwelling on Aamir's nakedness.

"There's nothing in the fridge," Noori said in despair as she ransacked the kitchen in search of food. Aamir was right by her side, momentarily distracting her from her rumbling tummy. He still smelled of patchouli.

"What about flour?" Aamir asked.

"Yup. They have that."

"Good. Breakfast is sorted then."

Aamir smiled. It was nice to see him show teeth.

30
aamir

Maa used to make rotis every weekend, mixing flour with salt and water, kneading the dough, and slicing it into neat balls that she rolled out and fried in a griddle, adding the finishing touch by brushing a generous amount of oily ghee on top.

That smoky smell of home-made flatbread took Aamir back to Pakistan and to the dusty Punjabi village, an hour north of Lahore, where he had last seen his mother. And here he was, eight months later, making rotis, watching them darken and inflate like balloons, the definite sign they had to come off the heat.

"Didn't think you'd be able to handle a saucepan," Mahnoor said with a sniff.

She plopped a generous dollop of butter onto a warm roti, letting it melt for two seconds before taking a big bite. That girl had an appetite. He had made four rotis, and she had wolfed down three of them.

"They're almost as good as my mum's, but they're missing a secret ingredient."

Aamir glanced up, grabbing roti number five. This one belonged to him.

"What's that?" he asked.

"Motherly love, of course." Mahnoor stopped chewing, coming to some kind of horrified realization. "I'm so sorry. My big mouth – I shouldn't have said that."

She fell silent, busying herself with grabbing two gold-rimmed cups and producing a carton of long-life milk from the larder that seemed to contain everything from dried pasta to soy sauce and heaps of white chocolate. The kettle came to a boil and Mahnoor proceeded to make tea the proper way, using a teapot.

Early-morning tea and rotis, was there anything better than this?

Yeah, good company.

"That thing I just said." Mahnoor licked a crumb off her lips. "About motherly love. That was dumb."

"But it's true."

Aamir could see her embarrassment. He wanted to take it away. No, Aamir would never feel that type of love again, but that wasn't Mahnoor's fault – she shouldn't have to hide what made her happy.

"It's OK," he said, stuffing the last bit of roti into his mouth.

Now full, he joined Mahnoor at the island worktop in this luxury kitchen that his mother would have felt lost and out of place in. She had loved her small loft kitchen with her pots and pans and thousands of glass jars that contained her own mixture of spices, and pulses, and rice, and her life. He looked around – everything about Mahnoor's life was different.

She sat opposite Aamir, clutching her cup. She had poured the tea and they both listened to each other's muteness, waiting for somebody to press the unmute button.

"She died last year," Aamir said eventually. "So it's been a while."

"But *a while* seems quite short, don't you think?"

"How so?"

"You still have to live the rest of your life without her, that's how. It feels like forever, and before you know it, two years have passed, and then five, and then twenty, and then you're really old, like in your thirties, and you still miss her, and you still don't feel whole because you've lost her, and there's only the memory of her, but that memory isn't good enough, it's fading, and you're asking yourself whether she was ever part of your life, and the life that you're living doesn't make sense without her, not one bit, and it hurts, and it kills you one day at a time."

Mahnoor stopped, breathless, and took a slurp of her tea.

"All I'm saying is … time is relative," she said.

OK.

Was Mahnoor still talking about Maa? He had watched her closely as she spoke. Her quick breathing, the way each word slipped over her lips, the painful movement of her mouth, the dullness in her eyes, the slight tremble in her voice, the sniff that she added in the end. No. She wasn't talking about Maa.

"Mai told me about your cousin," he said. "I'm sorry."

"Me too."

Aamir waited, sipping his tea. Mahnoor wasn't done talking; he sensed her need to speak, but he also felt her reluctance. Grief wasn't something you could pour into a morning cup of tea. Not everyone could handle it. In fact, most people couldn't. They didn't want to hear about it – they pretended death was an abstract idea, when actually life was abstract, and death was as real as it got.

"She was seventeen," Mahnoor said.

"Was she ill, or…"

"No. It was an accident. Actually, let's just call it an unfortunate incident. It was bad luck."

"Bad luck?"

"Yep. There's good luck, there's bad luck, and then there are snakes."

"Snakes?"

"Yeah, those scaly creatures, you know. They strike out of the blue and can cause chaos and destruction."

Mahnoor lowered her face, staring into her cup of tea. What did she see in those muddy waters? She put on this tough exterior, hiding her vulnerable side, but there she was, sitting opposite him and trying to keep it all in, containing all her grief in that single cup, drinking from it, one sip at a time, until she got to the bottom and found it empty.

Maybe she needed to spill that cup, tip it over. Wasn't that the better way to deal with one's emotions, allowing them to flow and not trying to keep them in? Well, that was rich of him. Aamir had no idea how to handle real emotions; it was part of the reason why he was sitting in Bristol with Mahnoor – which was kind of nice. He had meant what he said earlier, about having met her, and how that made him feel grateful, in a way. Aamir didn't even mind her flare-up of anger. It was real and raw, albeit a bit noisy.

"What was your mum's name?" Mahnoor asked, breaking the silence.

"Nadira."

"Wow."

Mahnoor was still gazing at her cup as if she could find some treasure in there. But the serious expression had been wiped off her face. She was almost smiling now.

"Like Jahangir's Nadira."

"Who?"

"Don't tell me you've never heard of the most tragic love story of all time?" Noori asked. "Forget Romeo and Juliet; Jahangir and Nadira are the real deal."

"And let me guess: one of them dies."

"Of course, that's what makes it so tragic. Their relationship was illicit, you see. Jahangir was known as Crown Prince Salim. And Nadira, or Anarkali as they call her these days, she was a commoner, a beautiful court dancer from Lahore. And Jahangir's cruel father, the Mughal emperor, put an end to their love, burying Nadira alive."

"Sounds like folklore to me."

"Man," Mahnoor said, shaking her head. "Myth or not, the story is epic. When I go to Lahore, I'll visit Anarkali's tomb, the ultimate token of her lover's love."

"There's a tomb?"

"Of course there's a tomb. Jahangir built it for the love of his life – what could be more romantic?"

"I don't know. The guy could have written a poem or something."

"A poem!" Mahnoor gasped. "Ask any girl: they'd all demand a tomb, not a lousy poem!"

Mahnoor was funny. She liked unicorns and schmaltzy stories and obviously didn't give a damn what people made of her appearance. One look at the popcorn on her messy turban said it all. But there was something special about her.

"You know what?" she said, glancing at the time. It was just after seven o'clock in the morning. "I'll educate you."

"It's too late for that."

"It's never too late, mark my words."

Mahnoor skipped off the bar chair, grabbing her cup of tea. It was still full.

"Follow me," she said.

31
noori

Noori wasn't watching the film. She was studying Aamir in secret. Nadira and Jahangir were quietly suffering in the background, singing about their woes, and every now and again they would stop singing and talk. Like Noori and Aamir, who didn't stop waffling to each other.

"This film is boring," Aamir complained.

Noori tutted. "You have no taste."

"Come on, we all know Bollywood productions are rubbish. And chauvinistic."

"I can't believe you just said that."

Noori rearranged her turban haughtily. This guy was unbelievable. But wait, was there a kernel of popcorn stuck in her fringe? She should definitely have a wash later. Even Doughnut was cleaner than she was after his morning bath with Aamir. The beagle had placed himself between Aamir and Noori, who had parked themselves on Mai's bedroom floor.

Noori's head rested against the bed post.

Why were the three of them sitting on the floor, watching Anarkali's plight on Mai's computer? They could take a proper seat, on Mai's bed, Noori thought, but that would be weird. It seemed inappropriate to share a bed with a guy she hardly knew (although she'd seen him naked), even with Doughnut acting as chaperone.

"You'd like the film if you understood the dialogue and the singing," Noori argued.

"I understand every word," Aamir said. "And I still don't like it."

"You understand Hindi?"

This was news to her. Granted, the two languages were similar – Urdu and Hindi – which had allowed Noori to binge on Bollywood films for years without having to switch on the subs.

"Sure I do," Aamir said.

"But you said you didn't."

"I don't speak the language these days, but I still understand everything."

"Interesting."

"My parents always spoke a mixture of Urdu and Hindi at home," Aamir said. "I picked it up from them."

"Are they from Pakistan?"

"India."

"Oh," Noori said. "With a name like yours, I thought your parents were Muslim, and probably Pakistani."

"My dad's Muslim, but why does it even matter?"

She could see it didn't matter to Aamir, but it did matter to Noori. It was like he was in denial, like he didn't care where he originated from. Not everyone was interested in their heritage, Noori had to admit. Maybe having one clear heritage made it easier to understand who you were.

Aamir must have sensed Noori's rumination mode. He fumbled with his hand, stroking Doughnut's back, maybe looking for comfort. Stop! She should stop doing that, trying to analyse him. Aamir produced a lot of complex data and she was most definitely not a data analyst. Noori diverted her gaze back to the screen.

"You know the best thing about Bollywood films?" he asked.

"The clothes?"

"Nope. The lack of sex scenes."

"Yeah, sex scenes are lame. So fake."

That sounded like Noori knew what she was talking about. She didn't.

"The clothes are cool, though; you're right," Aamir agreed.

"And the music."

He snorted. "Definitely could do without the music; it's like watching a Disney film."

"Bollywood, Disney, what else is on your hate list?"

"Hate is a strong word," Aamir mused. "It's overused. Like love."

"How can love be an overused word? Love is love."

"Exactly. How can people say 'I love macaroni cheese' and then say 'I love my children'? That doesn't make sense."

"I use love and hate all the time. Like, a few days ago I told my dad I hated him. Didn't go down well."

"I remember," Aamir said. "And do you really hate him?"

"Everyone knows that hating your dad equals loving your dad."

"Yeah, families are complicated. And parents always think it's their kids that are wrong, but—"

"They're the ones with issues." Noori spat. She was seething, everything bubbling inside her, desperate to erupt in a sea of angry lava.

"What did he do, your dad?" Aamir asked quietly.

"He betrayed me." Noori took a deep breath. "He called my auntie in Lahore and told her I was mentally unstable."

Aamir squinted, unsure what to make of those words. "Why?" he stuttered finally. "Why would he do that?"

"Because he's trying to sabotage my plans. He doesn't want me to go to school in Pakistan and he went behind my back, coming up with these elaborate lies to make it seem like I'm not *sound of mind*. He told my auntie I have mental health issues. I mean, what father does that? As if moving to a different country for a year would make me go nuts or something. He basically begged her to put an end to my trip because she's the one who got me into school there and I'll be staying at her place. But he didn't realize that the women in this family stick together. Of course she didn't believe him, and now I know that my dad only wants what's best for him, not for me."

Noori's eyes widened. She couldn't believe she had just said those words, almost vomiting them out. She felt sick and sad and furious, all at the same time. Aamir was frowning, unable to comprehend the weight of her unexpected revelation. Beneath her anger, she felt relief. Finally she had told someone. It even sounded a bit ridiculous saying it out loud, but it was the secret that had gnawed away at her, making her ashamed of her dad. He had portrayed his daughter as a hysterical madwoman, like one of those crazy old ladies in Victorian novels.

Noori didn't need her dad to speak for her. She had her own voice, and she wanted to be heard. Her father wanted to rob her of all of it; he wanted to take control of the narration when it was Noori's story to tell, Noori's life to live. Well, he could try all he wanted, but she'd hop on that plane to Lahore – just like Munazzah had.

Munazzah. Everything had changed since she was gone. Noori had changed. And more was to come; she could feel it in her bones. Munazzah had once said something clever about transformations. Noori wished she could remember, but that memory had faded, leaving only a vague feeling of comfort behind. Life had felt less chaotic when Munazzah was around. She had been a source of light, illuminating Noori's inner and outer world that had since been thrown into pandemonium.

The truth was, Noori wanted to be more like her cousin, who had been outspoken in a gracious yet shrewd way. Munazzah would have known what to do or say and how to behave, unlike Noori, who always seemed to try to figure out life by acting ungraciously. Noori missed her cousin and the way things used to be.

Bristol was different.

Her family was different.

Life was different.

And Noori felt tired, too tired to confront her dad about the lies he had told. Maybe her family did think she was bonkers; maybe the whole world thought she was mental. But why then did Noori feel that the world had gone mad and she was the only sane person left?

As her mind whirred a weird thought struck Noori. There was a *slight* silver lining to the whole situation. If she hadn't argued with her dad four days ago, she'd never have stormed out of the house and met Aamir, and she wouldn't now be sitting on Mai's bedroom floor, watching *Anarkali*. Strange how one incident could alter the whole direction of life.

Running into Aamir almost felt like *qismat* – fate. But Noori didn't believe in destiny and preordained encounters, not after what happened to Munazzah. Was her cousin's death meant to happen? Noori didn't think so. Munazzah's mortal encounter with that snake was one big cosmic cock-up that Rumi described as a "coming together" – somehow.

At times Noori truly felt that she couldn't take it any more. She was still here, in Bristol, where she had grown up with her cousin, and being here by herself didn't feel right. That was why she wanted to escape from this place, forget the memories, the pain. It was too suffocating to go to their school, to pass Munazzah's former home that had been sold to a young family, to chew their favourite cinnamon gum, to sit on her bench and wait. For what? Munazzah wasn't going to come back.

Noori glanced at Aamir, at his long hair, the fading bruise

on his soft cheeks, his round chin. He looked thoughtful – just on the edge of a question.

"So, are you running to or away from something by going to Pakistan?" Aamir asked gently, as if not to offend her.

Luckily Noori took no offence.

"Dude, I hate running, trust me. And why would I run if I can dance?"

Aamir nodded in amusement, kind of. She saw something else in his face, something she couldn't put her finger on.

"Have you talked to your father about the situation?" he asked. "You should probably give him a chance to explain himself."

Noori sighed. "I don't know. We'll just end up arguing, and the truth is, I don't like arguing. Really."

"An argument isn't always a bad thing, and it's not like he's going to kick you out of the house."

Aamir sort of smirked then. Was he trying to be funny? He had said those words with a lightness in his tone, as if he didn't care he'd been chucked out by his only living parent. He was good at masking his pain, but Noori was good at unmasking people.

"So why did your father do it, kick you out?" Noori said, unable to let this one go. "So you went off the rails for a bit – happens to everyone. That's not a reason to throw someone out of their home."

Aamir stared at her. Those huge eyes. Noori saw her watery reflection in them.

"Shame," he said, his voice a whisper.

32
aamir

"What do you mean by shame?" Mahnoor asked. "Is your dad super religious or something?"

"He thinks he's a mullah."

"A religious scholar?"

Aamir nodded.

Maybe Mahnoor didn't get the concept of shame, but Aamir did. He had felt ashamed for months. And he knew he had made a mistake. He shouldn't have run away from his problems and his grief. He had tried to numb that pain by getting drunk and doing other haram stuff.

He had felt bad about it, but it was the only way he could cope with the pain after Maa died. Aamir couldn't face the empty kitchen, the absence of her perfume, the soundless evenings – Maa had loved to watch her Indian films at night, falling asleep in front of the TV until Pa woke her and told her to go to bed.

Pa. Aamir couldn't forget the strained look on his face after Claire's impromptu visit. She'd won. She had been intent on getting her revenge ever since Aamir had broken off the relationship. She had loved Aamir and had told him that every day, in her clingy way, trying to own him. Perhaps Aamir should have let her down more gently. Perhaps he shouldn't have sent her a drunken text in the middle of the night, telling her in plain terms it was over. No – he shouldn't have done it like that. But the truth was they were both better off without each other.

When Maa had died, Claire had tried to be there for him, and he had pushed her away. He was dying inside. He was looking for comfort, and Claire wasn't the one who could give it to him. She didn't get him. Maa's death had opened his eyes, changed him forever. He didn't want to spend his time with a girl he had once liked, but never loved. Their relationship wasn't meant to last. Maa was right and Aamir had told Claire so, hurting her on purpose so she'd stay away.

That thing Maa had said about finding Aamir a wife when he was old enough... He had passed that info on, knowing Claire would feel offended, knowing his mother hadn't thought Claire was wife material. He wanted Claire to get angry so she'd leave him alone, and his plan had sort of worked.

"She'd have ruined your life," Claire had spat. "Your mum wanted to marry you off to some girl you don't love, and you'd have been OK with that, just because it's tradition and you're expected to go along with it?"

Aamir had nodded, in his grief, meaning it. Maa was dead, and her death showed him he would have done anything to please her had she lived, even if it meant signing up to the institution of marriage – although Aamir wasn't even sure he believed in it.

Claire didn't understand what it was like to grow up in a family like his. There was love, plenty of it, but there were also expectations. Bilal had fulfilled those expectations. He had studied, became a dentist, and married a woman from Pakistan, someone Maa knew.

Aamir's family had close ties to Pakistan. Some of the Mahmoods lived on the other side of the Indian border, near Lahore. Those relations were rich; they hadn't lost their livelihoods, hadn't fled all those years ago during the partition. Most of Pa's family were in Pakistan, and most of Maa's lot had escaped from Lahore to Amritsar, in India. Maa was Sikh but had converted. Pa was Muslim. Theirs had sort of been an interfaith marriage.

It was confusing.

His father had tried to instil his faith in him; his mother never did. She let him be. Claire never got that. Maa only wanted what was best for Aamir. When he had first told his mother about Claire, she had asked him one question: "You think she'll make a good wife?"

Aamir was taken aback. He was sixteen at the time, didn't dream of getting married. But Claire was his first girlfriend and he wanted Maa to know about her. He'd burst into laughter, thinking his mother was joking until he realized she was dead serious.

"I like Claire," he'd explained to Maa. "But I'm not thinking of marrying her."

"In this case, don't tell your father; he wouldn't understand," Maa had replied.

"Wouldn't understand what?"

"That you're still young," she'd said, leaving Aamir puzzled for a moment.

Maa had always known his relationship with Claire wasn't going to last, which was why she'd asked him not to tell Pa – to save Aamir from unnecessary trouble. Though that didn't quite work out.

"You know what?" Mahnoor said, staring at his grief-stricken face and cutting through his thoughts. "You can go to Cardiff or whatever, but that thing you were talking about – shame – it'll follow you. So, want to hear my free advice?"

"Go on."

"Life is short, and it's never too late."

"Too late for what?"

"To do the right thing."

Aamir thought about those words. Perhaps Mahnoor was right about shame following him around. But whatever Mahnoor was running from, it would stalk her too, all the way to Pakistan. He wanted to ask her more about those plans of hers. Why did she want to go to school in Lahore? What was waiting for her there? Wouldn't she miss home?

If he were to pose those questions, she would think he was questioning her choices – like her dad. Like his dad. Sometimes, he realized, questions didn't need to be answered. Sometimes, questions have no answers.

33
noori

He was so vulnerable, Aamir, that guy with the long wavy hair that he had twisted into a bun and that made him look so gorgeous. There. She had said it. She'd admitted the truth to herself. Not that he was her type. She wasn't into misfits in that way. She felt sorry for him, that's all.

She had so many questions, like what the hell was all this talk about shame? She longed to know, but then he might run away *again* and that would be it.

Doughnut, who had up till then been dozing with his head on Aamir's lap, jerked awake. He lifted his head, curled his ears, and rose to his furry paws. Off he went, down the stairs, Rumi knows where.

It was just the two of them now, and there was a gap where Doughnut had slumbered. Noori became aware of her breath, and his breath, the way his bulky chest rose as he inhaled. He wore a pair of brown chinos that he had rolled up to his ankles.

She took in his black shirt with a V-neck, the tan line on his arms, the fuzzy hair on his fingers.

"The right thing." Aamir mumbled, not taking notice of Noori's prying eyes.

"Yeah. That's all you have to do," Noori said, glancing away at his feet and his sporty ankle socks.

"I don't know what the right thing is."

"I guess you just have to swallow your ego and apologize to your father. Maybe he didn't mean to throw you out. Maybe he was just angry and said the wrong thing."

"Nah."

"Don't let shame stop you. What *is* it anyway?"

"It feels bad."

"And how does it feel now?"

"Pretty stupid," he admitted. "Because of it I ended up being robbed, and then I met you."

"Lucky you."

Aamir did this thing that Noori couldn't describe, didn't find the proper words for. He lifted his cheeks, and he was smiling without smiling. The wrinkle between his eyebrows disappeared. She detected a hint of amusement in his face, and it rested in the dark dimple on his chin.

He turned to gaze at her. She didn't look away. His eyes drifted to her lips. Her eyes drifted to his lips. Noori swallowed. Anarkali was still warbling in the background, drowning out Noori's flitting heartbeat. She felt it, that sensation in her tummy. It wasn't a fluttering butterfly. It was more like a sick, dying butterfly that was going to crash to the dusty ground any moment and die a slow, agonizing death.

"Mahnoor," he said, his voice a notch deeper than usual. "Thank you."

"Don't know what for, but you're welcome."

"You know why."

The butterfly was about to sign off, walk towards the light, give up the ghost.

"You offered me – a complete stranger – chai, and then lunch, and a place to crash, which means you're either bonkers…"

"Or?"

"Really nice."

Noori had to stop staring at his lips. They were nice too. Dark, and curled, and spotty. Right on his bottom lip, Noori spotted two brown dots. They looked like crumbs of plain chocolate, waiting for someone to lick them off.

Ding! The image popped back into her mind. She had managed not to think about Aamir in the bathtub for a while. There was nothing attractive about naked guys. Nothing whatsoever. Could he read her mind? Was the embarrassment written all over her flushed face?

"By the way," he said, "I know you saw me."

"Sure, I can see you right now."

"That's not what I mean."

Please, butterfly, die, or fly away; just leave me alone.

"I'm talking about the bathroom," Aamir said.

"All I saw was your head, I swear. I didn't peek; I mean I wouldn't. I'm not a perv."

"You're blushing."

"Listen," Noori said, in an attempt to kill the butterfly. "We should probably do something, don't you think? Can't sit around on the floor all day; my parents will be wondering where I am."

"Mahnoor."

Why did he have to say her name like that? She had to kick him out of Mai's bedroom.

"That thing you said about doing what's right – how do I do that?" he asked.

"OK," she said. "I'll translate it for you: go inside, listen, and then take action. Don't sit on your bum all day. There's a time for ruminating, and there's a time for … actionating. Let's practise: is there something you want to do right now?"

"There is."

"Good. Let's do it then."

Aamir frowned, looking like he had swallowed a fish whole, and a spiky one at that. He was sweating, and he was a tad pale. Maybe the fish he'd gulped down had given him food poisoning. Had she said something wrong? She always did; that was Noori's problem. Her tongue moved faster than her brain.

His lingering eyes were making her nervous, and Noori rearranged her pink turban in an effort to hide her nerves. Why was she even wearing a headscarf? Her identity crisis was a complex affair, and she had tried to solve it by putting on a headscarf. And here she was, preaching to Aamir, when she had no clue what she was talking about. Aamir must have known she was a fraud, the way he was examining her.

"There's only one thing I can think of doing right now,"

Aamir said, leaning in towards Noori.

Before she knew it, they were face to face. Noori was squinting at Aamir's forehead, at his inky eyebrows and the ridge of his nose. He moved fast and pinched something off the top of Noori's head. The gentle waft of patchouli, the breeze of breath on her cheeks. They locked eyes for a moment. He loitered there, in front of her, and Noori felt as if she were being pulled towards him, like the tide to the shore.

"Popcorn," he said, moving away, swift as a shadow. "It was stuck on your headscarf."

Noori swallowed.

What the hell had just not happened?

34
aamir

"Everyone should wear popcorn on their headscarves," Mahnoor said, adding a funny laugh.

She sounded nervous. Aamir's heart rate had stabilized again. He was gazing down at his feet, as if he had committed a sin when nothing had actually happened between them, other than that one single moment when the world stood still and they had almost brushed lips. He hadn't imagined it, the way her body had shifted to adjust to his, the way she'd watched him, inching closer. If he hadn't reacted and backed down, they would have…

"Popcorn prints on headscarves! Maybe that's the way to make them fashionable," she added.

"I don't think people consider the headscarf to be a fashion item," Aamir said, clearing his throat.

"How do you know?" she retorted, her voice rising as if a switch had been flipped.

The headscarf was clearly a sensitive issue. Four days ago, when they had met by the bench, she hadn't been wearing one. He had since wondered about the reasons that had motivated her to wear a headscarf and hadn't come up with a plausible explanation.

She was glaring at him, waiting for an answer. That girl could be scary.

"The headscarf," Aamir said, trying to think under difficult circumstances. "To most people it's not fashion but a sign of their belief systems."

"Says who? Some mullah, some *man*?"

"Men *and* women, yeah."

"I don't care what people think or say. I can wear a headscarf and treat it like any other piece of clothing."

"But sooner or later people will comment on the fact that you're matching a headscarf with shorts."

"What are you saying? I'm not chaste enough? You sound like those sexists who criticised Malala for wearing skinny jeans and heels!"

Aamir let out a sigh. What else could he do? There was no point arguing with her. She'd always think she was right. He hadn't meant to bring it up, the headscarf thing. It was a source of conflict, and Mahnoor's sudden anger, he believed, was probably a sign of insecurity. She didn't want people to question her choices, question who she was, because she was already doing that herself.

"You're wearing chinos," she said, pointing a sharp finger at his trousers. "That's what soldiers used to wear; that's where they come from. Are you a man of the military or are you just a guy who likes chinos?"

"You can't compare chinos with headscarves."

"Why not?"

"It's different. I like chinos because they're comfy and—"

"And I like my headscarf because it's what my ancestors wore; it's part of who I am and where I come from. Why should I hide that?"

"So it's a statement to reclaim, what, part of your heritage?" Aamir asked.

"Yes, maybe."

"And your shorts: do they represent your British heritage or..."

"I am mixed, so I can mix styles, all right?"

"That doesn't make sense."

"Why does everything have to make sense when nothing makes sense?" Noori paused, a mixture of fury and fear scribbled on her face. "It makes me feel closer to her."

"There you are!" someone said.

Mahnoor's mum, followed by Doughnut, trotted into the room. Where had they come from?

Aamir reluctantly tore his eyes from Mahnoor while shifting back to make space under the scrutiny of a mother who was inspecting the room and its inhabitants with curious caution. Had she picked up on the weird atmosphere?

"What are you two doing here?" Mahnoor's mum asked, giving Noori an interrogative look.

"The question is, what are you doing here, Mum?"

"I was watering the plants in the front garden when I saw Doughnut next door, running out of the house."

"He opened the front door again?"

"Yes, and so I checked up on things and found you two in here." Mahnoor's mum turned her head to glance at Aamir, who shuffled even further away from Mahnoor. "I'm surprised to see you, Aamir. I thought you'd left."

"He missed his train because he got mugged," Mahnoor said. "So I checked in on him; that's not a crime, is it?"

"Robbed? How awful! Are you OK?"

"It's nothing," Aamir said, watching Mahnoor gaze innocently at her mother. She had lied to her without lying. Impressive.

"Do you need checking over? I'm a doctor."

"Oh, no. I'm fine."

"And we'll have to call the police and report this abhorrent crime. I can't believe—"

"Calm down, Mum," Mahnoor said, rising to her feet and shutting down her friend's computer. "All Aamir needs is a cup of tea and he'll be all right."

And that was how one strange event led to another, and another, and another.

Hours later, when Aamir went to sleep that night, he wasn't dozing on a bench in the park or gazing at a vast night sky. Instead he stared at a plastered ceiling and a spider crawling across it. He was staying in a guest bedroom. There were clean towels, neatly placed on a plush armchair. His clothes had gone through a wash and were currently waiting to be ironed. He had been fed. He was almost happy.

But he knew his luck would run out soon. Aamir couldn't stay with Mahnoor's family forever. Her mother had insisted on giving him a medical check-up, wondering whether he had a concussion (from what he wasn't quite sure; maybe from being bashed up), as worried as if she were his mum. He had, with reluctance, told her about the pain in his chest that hadn't gone away in days, and she'd produced a stethoscope and listened to his heartbeat, hearing some kind of murmur that she suggested needed to be looked at properly.

Receiving that amount of unmerited attention made him feel shitty. Mahnoor's family had let him into their house, believing he was Mai's cousin. He had gained their trust by lying to them. And in all of this Mahnoor acted along. She'd become his accomplice.

Things were strange between them after the headscarf discussion and the popcorn moment. Something had definitely changed, but Aamir was too knackered to think any more about today's peculiar events and how he had let down his own family, while Mahnoor's had welcomed him. He was exhausted and he desperately needed sleep, to allow his body to recover from the past few days.

Aamir closed his eyes, and all he could see was her face.

DAY 5

35
noori

Seven o'clock. Noori lay wide awake in her cosy bed. All she could think of was Aamir, who was staying two rooms down from her, probably snoring in his sleep. There were a couple of thoughts that kept popping into her head.

One: Aamir naked. He was the first guy she'd seen in his birthday suit.

Two: Aamir was staying in her house, right now.

Mum was crazy; maybe that's where Noori got it from. After she had found Aamir and Noori next door, she had checked his vitals and said his temperature was a bit high. She'd then offered him breakfast and listened with genuine worry to his story of how he had been robbed, which wasn't a lie as such. And when she asked how he was going to get back "home" to Scotland, Noori chirped in, telling a real lie.

"His dad's sorting it out; he's going to book Aamir a train to Edinburgh."

Mum had frowned. "That's a long trip," she had said, before enquiring when Aamir was due to leave.

"Tomorrow," Aamir had replied, and Noori's heart felt like it had been filled with cement. So he was going to head off today, and then she'd never see him again, as she was moving to Pakistan in two days. It was … sad. Mum must have thought the same because she invited him to stay the night.

"What would you do all by yourself in that empty house?" she had asked, referring to Mai's vacant abode. "We've got a bed here, and food."

Food was very important to Mum. She more or less forced Aamir to stay, Rumi knows why. And so he had spent all of yesterday with the Oateses, helping Mum prepare lunch, playing a video game with the twins, reading one of Dad's history books in the garden under her father's watchful eyes. And Noori? She had avoided Aamir as best as she could and made sure not to spend any time alone with him. The last time the two had been on their own, they had almost smooched. Or maybe not. It could have been her imagination. Aamir probably wouldn't dream of kissing Noori.

What was that clinking sound?

It was coming from downstairs. Noori glanced at her bedroom door. Doughnut must have opened it while she was asleep and the beagle was probably in the kitchen, causing havoc. Noori toppled out of bed.

Fighting an urge to peep into Aamir's room, Noori tiptoed down the stairs, following the noise. It led her to the kitchen, where Doughnut was lying asleep on top of an old cloth and a pair of oven gloves that he must have torn down from the towel hook. The creature that was responsible for making the noise wasn't the dog, though. It was Aamir, who was in the middle of making himself a cup of tea.

He stared at Noori as if laying eyes on her for the first time. Aamir was fully dressed, unlike Noori, who was missing a headscarf. He looked sleepy, his hair sticking to his forehead, one hand loosely holding on to a book, the other gripping a cup of tea that he placed carefully on a coaster on the waxed table.

"Hello," Aamir croaked. His voice sounded funny, like he had a cold.

"Hi." Noori glanced at Doughnut. "I guess he woke you up?"

"Yeah, he barged in and jumped on the bed."

"Doughnut loves jumping on beds."

"Which makes it difficult to sleep," Aamir said with a yawn, placing the back of his hand over his chocolate lips. "So I decided to come down and read."

"That's one of Mum's books, right?" Noori asked, knowing the answer. She had seen this novel on the shelf for years, not once picking it up. Her mother kept all her books in the spare bedroom that used to be Munazzah's room when she stayed over. "What's it about?"

"The partition of India."

"Interesting."

Noori had to stop saying that word. It was lame, and made her sound stupid and unimaginative.

"Was your family affected by the partition?" she asked.

"You know, the splitting of one country, the mad butchering of an ancient land and its people, and the whole refugee crisis that followed when the Brits decided to give up their colonial reign after exploiting India for centuries, drawing random borders across the country, causing trauma and displacement and endless suffering and bloodshed."

Noori stopped to take a breath and felt her cheeks darkening. She had asked Aamir about his family again because she wanted to know everything about him. The sped-up history lesson? Who knew what that was.

Aamir glared at the window and the world outside, which was bathed in sunshine. She observed his hazy reflection in the glass. It was like a veil had been draped over his face, one that had to be lifted to see the real Aamir, who was constantly in hiding. From everyone. His mind was absent, she could tell. Had he even heard her question? Noori didn't think so.

36
aamir

Aamir knew she was watching him, the way he was watching her. Mahnoor's powerful presence was difficult to ignore. She was this bright bulb, and he was a shady moth, drawn towards its light and warmth.

She was waiting for an answer. She always wanted answers.

"Nineteen forty-seven," Aamir said.

"Huh?"

"The partition of India, the summer of nineteen forty-seven."

Should he tell her the family story, the one Maa had recounted many times, never able to forget what had happened so many years ago when she had not even been born? He could give away part of it, not the whole thing. Aamir cleared his sore throat. He felt a bit under the weather and took another soothing sip of tea.

"The train station in Lahore, it was blood-soaked back

then," he said, not looking at Noori. "My people, my family on Maa's side, they were Sikh and they all had to flee Lahore, their home town. When they got to the station they saw rows of dead bodies everywhere; the trains were filled with them. Somehow they managed to cross from what is now Pakistan into India, but I've no idea what happened to them on the way."

OK, so that wasn't true. Aamir knew all about it, had heard Maa relive the story of how her family had made that treacherous journey. Some of them had died, been murdered. And one five-year-old boy, Maa's uncle, vanished in the middle of the night. Nobody knew what happened to him. The family never recovered a body – they had lived with that open wound forever.

The story of the lost boy haunted Aamir. He'd seen a picture of him wearing a beautiful smile and a Punjabi patka, a turban. His name was Inayat. After Inayat became separated from his parents during a night of violence, they searched for him everywhere, but never found a trace of the child. Maybe someone picked him up and raised him; maybe he died the very hour he went missing. Everything smelled and tasted of blood then. Even the trees were bleeding.

And Maa had died because of Inayat. On their family trip to Pakistan, Maa had wanted to visit the place where, decades ago, her family had made that crossing to India, where they had lost little Inayat. And it was there his mother had met her end.

Her death could have been prevented. If they hadn't travelled to that quiet village near Lahore, they would not have run into the girl and Maa would have survived and Aamir wouldn't be in Bristol now talking to Mahnoor about a past that had snaked its way into the present.

Mahnoor was silent; she was studying him, peering at Aamir. She wasn't wearing her glasses; maybe that was why she was squinting so hard. And she wasn't wearing her headscarf either, not that he was going to mention it. Had she been wearing it to prepare for her journey to Pakistan? Who knew. After what happened yesterday, he'd keep his mouth firmly shut.

"What about your mum's family?" Aamir asked, trying to shake off his DNA and Mahnoor's omniscient gaze. "Did they have to move sides?"

"No," she said. "They've lived in the valleys of the Punjab for generations. I guess they were some of the lucky ones; they didn't have to run away."

"It makes you think," Aamir said.

37
noori

She had not seen him so sad, so lost in thought, so full of regret. Noori finally knew a bit more about him – about his family.

"It makes you think," Aamir repeated, as if murmuring in his sleep.

"Makes you think what?" she asked.

She held her breath, hanging on to his words, waiting in anticipation for his response. He flinched, as if he had just remembered something horrible. She couldn't bear his silence. She wanted to break it, so he would snap out of whatever was going on in his head.

Noori had to do something. She was overthinking again, waiting for Aamir to say or not say something. And why was she still standing? She should take a seat; this was her house, for heaven's sake! Would it be weird to plop down next to Aamir? Life was always full of difficult choices.

Aamir was seated at the kitchen table and there were five

free chairs. Noori didn't want him to think she was afraid of being close to him, or realize how nervous he made her, and so she did the only sensible thing that came to mind. She sagged into the seat next to him.

"Running away must be in my blood," Aamir said, out of the blue, unperturbed by Noori's proximity.

"The only thing that's in your blood is your blood," Noori scoffed.

"It's not that simple."

"Sure it is. Why make life more complicated than it is?" she asked, waiting for Aamir to finally look at her. "We're meant to live through chaos and pain, you know; we're not meant to run away from it, although it's tempting. I know all about it."

He coughed.

Were his eyes feverish or did Noori imagine it? Perhaps he was coming down with something. He shifted in his seat, his knee brushing hers. It was a casual "oh, I've accidentally touched your bare leg" moment, except Noori was thinking only one thing: *again*. Seriously, what was wrong with her? It was the tea in his eyes, the colour of his words, the taste of his presence, it was – everything.

Aamir turned his head her way, giving her one of his nondescript looks. It hadn't been a good idea to place herself so close to him. He was messing with her brain, sending her eighty-six billion neurons into one direction. His direction. She caught herself leaning in towards him and staring at his lips – they were parted, and moving. He was talking to her, which came as a mild surprise.

"Maybe we're not meant to run away from our troubles," Aamir said, picking up the conversation. "But the truth is, if my dad hadn't kicked me out, I'd have run away anyway."

"What? Why do you say that?"

"Because things changed after my mother died. Because my father thinks I'm a disgrace, and he's right. Just look at me. What am I even doing here with you and your family? It's crazy, and the craziest thing is I never tried to work things out with them. I mean, my dad's grieving and my brother's grieving and we're all grieving, but not talking to each other. And let me tell you, the not talking bit leads to all sorts of misunderstandings. I realized that with Claire."

Who the heck was Claire, and why did her name cause Noori to feel a mild to extreme sense of irritation?

"Claire and I," Aamir said, "we never talked about anything meaningful, and we just kept hurting each other. She hates me now. And she came up with that abortion story, a plain lie, telling my dad about it, and my dad didn't even know I had a girlfriend because I wasn't supposed to have a girlfriend. I was supposed to go to the mosque and pray and learn the Quran by heart although I don't understand a single word of it. I never listened to him; I did all the wild stuff I wasn't meant to do. I'm the son he lost a long time ago; I never fitted in, you know? Sometimes running away is for the best."

Aamir's face hardened and then softened when he saw Noori's round eyes growing rounder. She was taking this all in, bit by bit, analysing every part of his story: Aamir, grieving the loss of his mother, never got on with his father (note: religious/cultural differences?). Aamir, doing wild stuff in his past (drugs, alcohol, girls? tbd). Aamir, having an ex (fake abortion story??). Why, out of all the things he had just revealed, did this last point bother Noori the most?

She had to say something. He was staring at her and all she could come up with was "Oh." Aamir didn't look impressed by Noori's curt reply. The frown was back. She had to think fast, otherwise Aamir would clam up again.

"And now?" she said, feeling dumb as a brick.

"Now what?"

"What are you going to do?"

"Dunno."

"Have you thought about what I said?" Noori asked, knowing Aamir was closing down after his unexpected outburst. "That you could go back, apologize, say sorry to your dad, your girlfriend—"

"My *ex*?" Aamir curled his fists into balls. "Are you kidding? She made up an abortion!"

Noori inadvertently flinched, not out of fear – clearly the lie was still a sore point – but from slight indignation. He was blatantly ignoring his part in all of this.

"Anyway, they don't want anything to do with me," he said.

"Bollocks, you're just scared."

"My dad wouldn't forgive me. And I'm dead to Claire."

"I'm sure that's not true. You must have, uh, you know." Noori needed to get this right. She tried again. "You must have loved her at one point."

"Love? No, never loved her, but I guess I shouldn't have broken up with her by text."

"You did *what*?"

Noori had no right to judge Aamir, but she did. So far, she had thought he was a decent bloke, and not an arse who'd hang out with a girl he didn't love only to dump her via text. That's what had happened to Mai, and it had taken her months to recover.

Noori didn't hide her dismay, her face a blend of shock, fury and disappointment. She was a big believer in sisterhood. She didn't know Aamir's ex, but he had clearly broken her heart – and broken hearts were no fun.

"Why are you looking at me like I'm evil?" Aamir asked.

"Because you are," Noori said. "No guy, or girl, should break up with their partner by sending them a *text*. That's what jellyfish do."

"Excuse me?" he said with an incredulous stare.

"It's spineless!" Noori clarified.

"Look, it's not like Claire was an angel. She lied."

"Because you broke her heart! What did you expect? That karma only works one way? Every action leads to a reaction."

"Oh, so it's OK she made my dad believe I got her pregnant?"

Noori was trying to temper her temper. This wasn't her business, but she still felt a weird sense of betrayal. It was her own fault. Aamir was a virtual stranger. He was a coward, and she was a cow. She should stay on her patch of grass, and he on his – no boundaries crossed, no bad feelings. But cows like to stray, don't they?

"For a person who reads Rumi, you're pretty ignorant," Noori said. "I'm not saying your ex is innocent and I'm not saying your father is without guilt, but I'm saying you can be an idiot."

"Gee, thanks." Aamir took an angry gulp of tea.

"Go to Cardiff, whatever. Run away from everyone who cares about you, me included." Noori forced herself to hold Aamir's stony gaze. Had she just told him she cared? Man, she was such a moron.

38
aamir

Mahnoor was annoyed, and frankly so was he. Also, Aamir was feeling *rough*. His neck was hot; his eyes were burning. He was definitely coming down with something and no wonder. Those nights sleeping outdoors hadn't been the warmest. His bones felt heavy and his body was beginning to ache in the weirdest places. In his toes, and coccyx, and thumbs. And then there was this dull ache in his chest; it was getting worse each day.

Mahnoor gave him her trademark glare. He shouldn't have told her a thing. That girl gave him a headache, literally. Why the hell was he even getting into this with her? She didn't know him. They were strangers with different lives and different paths and—

"You know what, forget this," Aamir said, moving to get up. He needed to stop all this hanging around. It didn't matter what she had just said; he needed to *leave*.

Mahnoor's face crumbled for a moment until she regained

her composure. He stared at her: the eyebrows she didn't bother to pluck, the prominent sideburns, the pointy chin, the huge eyes, and he thought to himself: *beautiful*.

"I should go," he murmured, trying to keep his thoughts in check.

"All right!" Mahnoor agreed crossly. "Thank God you'll be out of this house, and my life, for good then. It's not like I needed you to waltz in. I have plenty of other things going on right now, and you just complicated everything by sleeping on my bench."

"Why are you always acting so petulant?" Aamir asked. "You think you're right and everyone else is wrong. What have I done to earn your anger now? I should be the one feeling annoyed, not you."

"Right. Whatever you say, Aamir."

"There, you're doing it again, making me feel like an arse," he complained, "and I haven't even done anything to you, have I? None of my problems are your problems."

"I agree with you on that one. You definitely have problems," she said. "Big problems."

"Oh, and you, miss she-who-knows-*everything*, don't?"

"You sound like my parents."

They stared at each other with stunned disbelief. Aamir was surprised Mahnoor was able to get to him. He shouldn't care about her opinions or what she made of him. He shouldn't feel the need to explain himself and yet he did.

"It's time you came down off your high horse and admitted your mistakes," Mahnoor said in a taut voice.

He narrowed his eyes, feeling his blood heat up with irritation and something else – something more profound. Mahnoor shrugged her eyebrows. She was waiting for him to speak.

"I know my mistakes, believe it or not," he said. "I know I should have treated people differently. My ex, my family. They could do with an apology, and there's nothing stopping me from picking up the phone and calling my dad to say sorry but…"

"So why don't you?" Mahnoor asked, sounding a tad less hostile. "You can use the landline, no problem. You can tell them what happened. They're your family; they'll listen."

"How would you know? You've never met them; you have no idea what they're like."

Mahnoor rolled her eyes. "You're a coward, like my dad," she said. "He voted leave during Brexit, you know. And now he has regrets! Such a pathetic guy."

Wait, what was she on about now?

"I didn't vote leave," Aamir said. "I had to leave my home—"

"Without trying to reconcile first? Every relationship encounters problems, but it's this whole bloody idea of being a sovereign body, isn't it? People voting against other people based on their differences, so they can make their own laws and build more borders because the world is such a threatening place and—"

"Are we still talking about me or Brexit?"

"Both!"

"You can't exactly compare me to a Brexiteer; I didn't even have the right to vote during the referendum."

"But you have a right to vote *now*; you can still change your mind – nothing is set in stone."

"I'm not like you!" Aamir spat out.

Was it the fever or was Mahnoor to blame for the drowsy heat in his head? She made him so hot and bothered. She always wanted to impose her opinion on people. But sometimes she needed to know when to keep back instead of holding others to her high and mighty moral code. This was *exactly* why he had decided to avoid people and relationships. He was supposed to be a lonely island.

"And do you want to know why?" Aamir asked, ignoring Mahnoor's startled face, her round eyes and parted lips. "Because, for one, I hate Bollywood films, OK?" She frowned, looking confused. "For someone who's all about *diversity*, it's amazing you can't see how the whole film industry has a serious problem with representation. And that's what you're looking for, right? To show that you're here representing *our* culture? You said so yourself. I mean, that's why you put on that headscarf, which is a complete joke. You have no idea what it means to wear a headscarf. You think it will solve your identity crisis?"

The moment Aamir began his rant he was hit by regret. He shouldn't have said that. He could see the damage his sudden bout of anger had caused as Mahnoor recoiled, eyeing him with alarm. Aamir was not the confrontational type. He tried to avoid conflict; he ran from it; he didn't want to get caught up in unnecessary emotions. But now … the conversation had spun out of control. *She* made him lose control. It was none of his business what Mahnoor got up to, and yet they *had* meddled in each other's business. He ought to say something, anything, to take the edge off things. But he wasn't good with words. Obviously.

Mahnoor scratched her head, lowering her gaze. She didn't look at him for a moment, as if she was having a conversation with herself, trying to figure out what to do or say to him.

"We're more alike than you think," she said in a flat voice, her cheeks flushing like a dark powdery rose. "We're both running from our problems. We're both struggling to figure out who we are by doing stuff that's not us. You by alienating everyone you love. And me by wearing a headscarf. It's all an experience, maybe an unnecessary experience, but how else are you going to realize who you are? By making mistakes that you try and correct, even if it hurts your bloody ego."

She stopped herself. Was she feeling embarrassed? Mahnoor hadn't lied when she said she cared about him. Why else would she get so furious with him, challenging him all the time? But then, he hadn't said it back. Aamir hadn't told Mahnoor he cared about her.

"And for the record," Mahnoor added, "I never said Bollywood was perfect. Nothing and no one is perfect. I have a big mouth, I know, but you?" She gave him a long hard stare that made him shiver. "You're still a coward."

Aamir thought briefly about trying to laugh it off but instead he cleared his itchy throat. She had a point.

"That's what Maa used to say," he admitted. Maa had never had any problem with pointing out his flaws.

Mahnoor sniffed. It was a self-righteous sniff. A slightly appeased, self-righteous sniff. "What happened to her?" she asked, her voice sounding softer than before.

"You mean, how did she die?"

Mahnoor nodded. Another change of direction. This seemed to be typical Mahnoor. But perhaps the mention of Maa had brought on a wave of empathy. Maybe they were both keen on clearing the air.

"It was an accident," he said. "A freak accident of nature. I was there when it happened. A snake – it bit her."

"A snake?" Noori's cheeks paled. "A *snake?*" she said again, unable to disguise her horror.

"I know. What are the chances of that happening? Been asking myself that question for months."

"Up to one hundred and thirty-eight thousand people die from snake bites each year," Noori whispered, her chin lowered, her eyes fluttering in disbelief.

"How – *why* – do you even know that?"

"My cousin," she said. "It happened to her."

Aamir studied her. She wasn't taking the piss; there was no trace of cruelty. She wasn't doing a Claire but...

"Are you being serious?" he asked.

"She's dead; of course I'm serious."

"That," he muttered, trying to find the right words but failing, "is a really strange coincidence." They seemed empty.

Aamir was freaked out. How was this even possible? They had both lost a member of their family because of a snake – a snake! The chances of that happening were so unlikely, and yet… In that unlikely something he had met someone who could relate to him on so many levels. His head was all woozy. This could not be real. This was the kind of crap you got in a Bollywood film, not in real life.

"There are no coincidences," Mahnoor said. "The world's a random place and sometimes two random people run into each other and hit it off; another time two random creatures meet and one of them, a snake or whatever, kills the other."

Her voice broke. Her eyes went blank.

Aamir thought about Mahnoor's words. Maybe she was right. The world was so chaotic and random. If Maa hadn't decided to visit that village she wouldn't have died. They had gone for a leisurely stroll, a few days after Bilal had got hitched in Lahore. It was early in the morning, the weather was perfect, and the two of them were in the countryside, visiting his great-grandmother's birthplace.

There was a girl; they had met her on a dusty path near some rice fields. Maa had pointed out a palm tree when the girl passed, smiling at him. That had taken Aamir by surprise. During his short stay in Pakistan, Aamir hadn't seen any girls smile in public at strange males. She didn't strike him as a local, and they must have been around the same age. The girl was on her own, except for a German shepherd that trotted beside her.

The dog barked, growled and went for something nestling under a shrub. Then all of a sudden the canine yelped, its eyes panicky, the girl in distress. Maa rushed to help, and both women were kneeling down next to the wounded dog when the snake appeared, sly, brown and yellow. At first Aamir didn't realize they had been bitten; then he didn't understand it was venomous until Maa asked him to fetch help. He rushed off, leaving Maa and the girl and the dog behind. But it was too late. He was too late. The viper killed them all. And that was how messed up life could be.

Mahnoor was staring at him. She had at least regained some colour.

"My cousin, she had a heart condition," Mahnoor said. "They think that's why she died. It must have been painful."

"I don't know." Aamir swallowed hard, trying to get rid of the lump in his throat. "Sometimes it can happen very fast."

"Was your mum… I mean, was she in pain?" Mahnoor asked quietly, her eyes glued to his face.

It would be so easy to lie; it would make her heart a lot lighter to believe in a lie. All he had to do was tell Mahnoor what she wanted to hear: something to soften the grief. Aamir could barely breathe. His nose was bunged up and his eyes were all watery. He had a cold, that was all. He wasn't close to tears. He would be OK.

"Maa wasn't in a good state. In the end," he whispered.

Mahnoor nodded, as if she'd known the answer all along. She deserved to hear the truth.

"At least they're both OK now," she said. "Wherever they are, they're OK."

"Yeah."

And now he was back to telling lies. He didn't think Maa, or Mahnoor's cousin, or the girl with the German shepherd, or the German shepherd, were OK. They were all gone. Forever.

39
noori

Noori knew Munazzah was dead, yet she was convinced that death was more like a rebirth. Aamir clearly didn't think so. But Noori felt her cousin's presence all the time.

"You don't believe me, do you?" she asked.

"Believe what?" Aamir said, his voice a croaky whisper.

"You think they're dead, your mum and my cousin."

Aamir gave her a calm yet confused stare.

"I don't think they're dead," he said. "I know they are."

"You can be dead and alive, just like you can be alive and dead."

"That doesn't make sense."

"What makes sense to you then?"

"Nothing."

"There must be something you believe in."

Aamir studied Noori's face.

She couldn't handle that type of attention, not from him.

She felt her cheeks burn like soft marshmallows, felt her brain melt like – uh – soft marshmallows. That boy had it in him. When he'd had a go at her a few minutes ago, criticizing her choice to wear a headscarf, questioning her beliefs and her obsession with Bollywood, she knew she'd found an equal.

Noori valued honesty. OK, she had initially been offended, but then her respect for him had begun to grow. In a weird way, she'd enjoyed their headbutting moment. Noori loved to fight – it was in her blood; and Aamir wasn't that different from her, even if he'd claimed he was. And then there was that revelation about the snake. It had floored her. She had a moment then, flipping out in her head, trying to calculate the chances of meeting someone else who had been affected by a snake bite in that way, but then he distracted her again. He always did that.

Aamir was throwing her that same intense look, like yesterday, when they were sitting on Mai's bedroom floor enjoying a moment of intimate stillness and his eyes had remained in one place, stuck on her.

"What are you looking at?" she asked, maybe sounding a tad defensive.

"You."

"It's weirding me out."

"I was thinking," he said, still weirding her out. "About what you said – whether there's something I believe in."

"Let me guess: you believe in nothing."

"I believe in one thing," Aamir said, still holding her gaze. "I believe in good people."

"What's that supposed to mean?"

"It means," he said, "that there are decent people out there who'll help you for no reason. And that's pretty cool."

"It's also pretty rare."

"I don't think so." Aamir's voice sounded coarser than before. "I met you."

Noori's heart stopped. She had to be careful now and reconfigure her brain. It felt like they'd gone from laughter to anger to sorrow and everything in between in a blink of an eye. She had to concentrate, but all she could think of was Aamir, and how he made her feel something she hadn't experienced before. In honesty, she felt a bit drained. He sapped her mind.

"You and your family have been very kind to me," Aamir said, serious as ever.

"Well, you're not the first creature I've picked up off the streets," Noori said. "There was a baby blackbird I found on the pavement, and a lost kitten I once brought home. We adopted them, but the cat ran away and the bird died. It was sad."

Aamir said nothing. He probably thought she was talking rubbish, but once your brain goes into gooey marshmallow mood, nothing intelligible can come from it. She had to say something less stupid and compensate for his nerve-wrecking silence.

"So what do you think?" Noori said, changing the topic like a pro. "Do you want to call your dad or your brother to let them know you're OK?"

"I don't."

"Do you believe in second chances?" Noori asked.

"Yeah, but…"

"I gave you a second chance and I'd even give you a third chance, although that would be pushing it. What I'm saying is, I'm not your family, thank God – hold on, that's not what I meant – anyway, I'm not related to you and, still, I've given you the opportunity to redeem yourself. I'm pretty sure your people will do the same if you take one tiny step in their direction."

"You gave me the chance to redeem myself?" Aamir was giving Noori a half-grin. "How so?"

"No point dwelling on the past. Shall I get the phone?"

Noori did not wait for a response. The moment she didn't inhabit the same space as him, she felt more like herself. But deep down, Noori had a bad feeling.

Aamir had done something to her brain, and the brain is connected to the heart. After the phone call, Aamir would pick up his backpack and head home to his family and they'd never see each other again, which would cause all kinds of regrets and emotions. She'd ruminate about him in the future, wondering how he was, where he was, and if he ever thought about her – in the middle of the night or while eating breakfast or staring at some clouds.

Noori's heart began to sink as she handed him the phone.

40
aamir

"My brother's not answering," Aamir said. He hoped Umaira and the baby were OK.

"What about your dad?"

"I can speak to my brother; that's about doable. But I'm not going to phone my father."

He had told Mahnoor about his last encounter with Bilal, even admitting how he'd walked out, not listening to Bilal's calls to wait. What would his brother have said anyway? That he needed to come back right this minute and treat Pa with more respect, apologize, and admit to each of his faults when they were all complicit in letting their family fall apart?

But maybe Mahnoor was right, and he shouldn't have taken off like that. Pa's sudden appearance had rattled him, yet still, it was no excuse for his cowardice. Aamir hadn't even had the guts to ask Bilal whether he could stay. His brother hadn't been in the right frame of mind, he could see that now. Bilal had had other concerns. And all Aamir had done by showing up when he did was add to that pile of worries.

Aamir sighed and followed Mahnoor into the conservatory. She had changed her clothes while he had tried to call his brother. The headscarf was back. They both sat cross-legged on the settee, their knees almost touching. He was thinking of shifting in his seat just so he could brush her shin again. But that made him feel a bit desperate. And as it was, he was still feeling off colour.

She was so close though.

"So why are you really wearing a headscarf? All of a sudden, I mean," Aamir asked, blaming his light-headedness for his idiocy. He shouldn't ask, but he couldn't resist; and anyway, she had heard all about his family, his mistakes, his transgressions.

Mahnoor shrugged. She wasn't in confrontation mode any more, or so it seemed.

"Look," she said, as if she were talking to a toddler. "Everything we wear is a marker of our identity. This thing, on top of my head, it's no different. I can be British and wear a headscarf. I can be Pakistani and not wear a veil. I'm figuring out the details."

Mahnoor was so unlike all the girls he'd met. Her dress style was … interesting. Her views weren't sugar-coated and her general attitude could be too much but refreshing all at the same time. Aamir wouldn't have given Mahnoor a second glance if he'd run into her a year ago, a month ago, a week ago.

Now, he couldn't take his eyes off her.

After a moment of silence, she turned to face him.

"Do you want to play a game to pass the time, until you get through to your brother?"

"A game?"

"Yeah. How about a knowledge game. I quiz you; you quiz me. On anything. Current affairs, films, the secret life of peacocks, you get it."

"All right." He struggled to find a question, suffering from brain fog. "What is the capital of Canada?"

"Ottawa."

"Is it? I thought it was Toronto."

Mahnoor rolled her eyes, shaking her head. "Nope, this is no good – you'll need to up your game!"

"There aren't many things I'm good at."

"Man, you need to get a grip. First you're saying you're a nobody, and now you're saying you're not good at this and that and blah. You've got to work on your self-esteem."

"But I am a nobody; we all are," he argued.

"Wrong. Split up the word *nobody* and you'll realize it's made up of two compounds. There's *no* and *body*. No body. As far as I can tell, you are in possession of a nice body." Mahnoor's eyes widened. "I didn't mean it like that," she stuttered. "I mean, you know what I mean."

"OK."

"It's not like I'm checking you out."

"You did yesterday." Aamir smirked – this girl was so easy to wind up.

224

"What?" Mahnoor protested, her voice a pitch too high. "I didn't see anything."

"Look me in the eye and say that again."

Mahnoor looked him in the eye, but she couldn't say a word.

41
noori

They were sat face to face, heart to heart, shoulder to shoulder. Noori didn't blink. Aamir blinked once, slowly, as if to check whether she was really there. And Noori had to make sure she wasn't hallucinating, because the longer she ogled Aamir, the closer he moved towards her. Or maybe it was Noori who inched forward, unable to resist his magnetic pull.

His eyes, she couldn't stop gazing into them. A weird thought popped into her head, and she considered sharing it with Aamir. But if she were to speak now, she might break the spell, and he'd look away and the magical moment would be over. Yet she had to do *something*. She couldn't spend the whole day gaping at him like a bloody moron.

"I," she said, concentrating hard on her words. "I read about a study once."

"Hmm?" The spell was still very much intact.

"They asked two strangers to gaze into each other's eyes for a couple of minutes."

"And. What happened?" Closer still.

"They fell in love. Pathetic, don't you think?"

"No."

Noori wanted to explain the scientific aspects of eye contact, a powerful stimulator of love and affection. When you stare at someone long enough, the body produces a chemical called phenylethylamine, and this chemical may make a person feel all lovey-dovey. But now, all she was able to get out of her mouth was a muddled mess.

"Ph-phenyl," she murmured, stuttering.

"Huh?"

Aamir looked all serious, but he wasn't frowning. This was a different kind of serious. He didn't give her the "what are you on about" stare. His eyes were feverish. And his cheeks were glowing and ruddy. He looked sick, like he was going to faint or something. Maybe he needed to see a doctor. Noori would ask her mum to give Aamir another check-up later. He could probably do with a good dose of medicine.

"You don't look completely … OK," she said.

Aamir didn't respond, and without giving it a second thought, Noori bent forward and placed a firm hand behind his neck to check his temperature. His skin was warm, but not hot. Noori didn't realize how far she had leaned into him, and now they were eye to eye again, breathing into each other.

And that's when it happened.

Her very first kiss.

French kiss, that is.

The phone was ringing, but neither of them paid any attention.

This moment belonged to them.

42
aamir

They didn't get to establish their parameters because moments later Mahnoor's dad darted into the conservatory and they sprang apart. He didn't seem pleased to see them. His face resembled the inside of a watermelon, including the freckly seeds.

"You're in trouble, young lady," Mahnoor's dad said, before glaring at Aamir. "And you too!"

Mahnoor didn't seem too disturbed by her dad's deepening red hue, though Aamir couldn't help but notice the accompanying vein pulsating in his neck. Aamir swallowed. It didn't surprise him that Mahnoor was in trouble. She was the kind of person who attracted and relished trouble, but what did it have to do with him? Well, a lot actually – the past few days were swiftly replaying in his mind. What had her dad found out?

"Guess who just phoned?" the father asked, glaring at his daughter.

"Dunno. Your great-aunt from Prague?"

"Our neighbour, the dear Mrs Vong!"

"Oh. Mai's mum," Mahnoor said, shifting in her seat as if a cactus had pricked her thighs. "How's France?"

"How's France? Are you kidding me? How about an explanation?" The father was struggling to breathe, and his enraged eyes were fixed on Aamir. "*Who* is this person?" he asked, pointing an aggressive finger at him. "He's not related to Mai, that much I know. And if you thought I ever bought that illegal adoption story, you must think—"

"Dad. You need to relax," Mahnoor said almost pleadingly.

"Mai's mum didn't sound relaxed when I told her about the distant cousin who doesn't exist!"

"OK," Mahnoor said, shooting Aamir a desperate look. "The cousin story was a lie, but—"

"Give me a straight answer! Who is this boy who's been sleeping in our house?"

She paused and bit her lip. How should you describe someone you just snogged to your mad father?

"He's a friend," she said, sounding defensive again.

And that was when Aamir's survival instinct kicked in. All he could think of was running away. That was his standard approach to dealing with conflict, unlike Mahnoor, who seemed to be actively seeking it. This father–daughter meeting was going to get nasty and Aamir would only make it worse if he stayed.

"I should leave," Aamir said. "I'm sorry, Mahnoor."

"Sorry?" the father asked. "What are you sorry for? Have you done something to my daughter?"

"Dad, I don't like your tone," she said, before turning her head towards Aamir. "And, Aamir, you don't have to go. You were going to try calling your brother again; he might be home now."

"It's OK. I can go back to his flat and—"

"What's this all about?" Mahnoor's father was shouting now, making Doughnut jump.

"Dad! I'm trying to talk to Aamir, so will you shut up for one moment? You're scaring Doughnut."

Mahnoor's father finally lost his cool, battling with wild hand gestures and words that he threw at his daughter, who retaliated by calling him a hypocrite and a back-stabber. That was over the top, even for Mahnoor.

Mahnoor's dad stopped his tirade, blinking at his daughter in confusion. Aamir had never seen Mahnoor so furious. But her behaviour was beginning to make sense, kind of. If that was how she viewed her father, no wonder she acted out – the headscarf a clear case in point. There was fire in her eyes and she was ready for battle.

Aamir caught some of their words as he scuttled away out of their lives. And that was when he realized he really was a nobody, and he owned nothing and no one, except his battered backpack.

43
noori

"What did you just call me?" Dad asked, taking a step back as if examining Noori from a distance would help him better understand his child.

He didn't get Noori and maybe he had a right to be angry with her – the cousin lie had been pretty stupid, and she probably shouldn't have called him a back-stabber – but then again, Noori felt entitled to be furious. The old man had interrupted Noori's first kiss, plus he was so full of double standards and *always* believed he was right. Noori knew she had inherited this trait from her father – her mum made sure to point it out constantly – and that made it even worse.

Noori bit her tongue. She wanted to call him out on so many things, but if she was going to win this battle, she needed to stay in control of her rollercoaster emotions.

"I know you called Auntie Shaima and said that going to Pakistan would cause me to *deteriorate*. You told her I was a nutcase."

"What?" His face was ashen, his lips set tight. He had not expected that. "I never said that."

"It's what you meant. And it doesn't change the fact that you lied so you can get your way. You don't care about what I want; all that matters is what you want." Noori sounded deflated. She was so angry she wanted to cry, and she hated angry crying.

"Of course I want what's best for you, but I don't think going to Pakistan will help you process what happened to Munazzah. You'll be away from us and what you need is—"

"What I need is not what you think I need," she countered. "You should *have* my back and not go behind my back. Why would you tell *my* relatives that I'm mentally fragile when that's not true?"

"I mean…" He faltered, frowning as if he didn't understand Noori's question. "I think you need to be in a familiar place right now; you need to be at home with us, because we're your safety net, and going off to Lahore by yourself will be challenging and, frankly, I don't think you're ready to handle this kind of change."

He spoke with a stern voice, but she heard the sorrow in her father's tone. Slowly he lowered himself onto a bouncy IKEA chair, heaving out a big sigh.

"Look," he went on, glancing at her headscarf again. "I know you're impulsive and rebellious – you get that from me, believe it or not – but if you're honest with yourself, you know that moving to a different country at this point in your life is not sensible."

Noori was only half listening. He hadn't answered her question and, judging by his response, her father obviously did believe she was fragile and in need of his protection. Underestimating her as always.

They looked each other in the eye. This discussion wasn't over, but she wasn't about to go off on another rant with Aamir around.

As if on cue, her dad spoke, scanning the room.

"Where's your friend?" he asked.

Noori, who had been too engrossed in her battle, turned around.

Aamir wasn't there. She could have checked the kitchen or the spare bedroom to see if he had simply moved to a different part of the house, but deep down she knew he had left.

Aamir was gone, and this time he wasn't going to come back.

DAY 6

44
aamir

Aamir was thinking of five things, his thoughts going round in a circle.

1. That kiss – perfect.
2. Mahnoor – she was not perfect, but he liked not perfect.
3. The fever – it had taken hold of him.
4. Water – he was thirsty.
5. Bilal – when could he next talk to him? Just to apologize and ask if Umaira was OK.

He dwelled the most on numbers 2, 3 and 5.

Mahnoor. Surely she must hate him, him leaving like that. But the feelings she had triggered in him scared him. He tried not to think about her, but the harder he tried, the harder he failed. Aamir had only known her for six days and although he couldn't claim to know her well, he felt a real connection to her.

A couple of times he had sneaked past her house to check if her parents were out, but there was always a car parked outside their gate that he assumed belonged to her mum or dad. He'd even made his way to the bench yesterday afternoon, hoping Mahnoor would turn up looking for him. She hadn't.

And yet.

He had to see her again, not only to pick up his only picture of Maa, which he'd somehow, stupidly, left behind. Was he making a habit of forgetting stuff at Mahnoor's place on purpose? Was some subconscious part of him eager to see her again? The answer to the last question was yes. He had to take one more look at Mahnoor to find out if seeing her one last time would change anything. He couldn't get that girl out of his head, and even Aamir, with his limited understanding of emotions, knew what that meant.

Back to number 5. Bilal. He'd scribbled a note and pushed it through Bilal's letter box, letting his brother know he was OK and asking if he could leave a spare key under the doormat outside the flat. And ever since, Aamir had traipsed around the harbourside, returning regularly to check the mat, hoping Bilal would come back to shower at some point and find his note. Until then he had to stay put. It was not like he had much choice.

There was no way Aamir could head back to Cardiff in the state he was in: number 3. He felt like crap. Something was wrong. At one point he had almost blacked out, but then he imagined Maa gently tucking his hair behind his ears, the way she used to whenever he was sick. That pain in his chest wasn't going away. It was getting worse with each step, each breath, each heartbeat.

Where would Aamir be now if Bilal had answered the phone yesterday? The whole situation was crazy, obviously, which was why he had spent some time by the bench, praying Mahnoor would miraculously appear like the first time they met, sort of saving him. He'd even fallen asleep on it, and didn't mind. His body must have become accustomed to the outdoors by now. The night had been warm, but his face had been hot. It still was. He was definitely running a high temperature and he could feel the heat in his head and his sore eyes. Why was he so short of breath, wheezing like a beached walrus?

Water. He could drink a gallon and he'd still be thirsty.

He pulled out his Rumi book, opening a page at random.

"Not only the thirsty seek the water, the water as well seeks the thirsty."

45
noori

Noori had her head buried under the cover when she heard a gentle knock on the door. With all her heart she wished it were Munazzah. Her cousin used to knock like that. She'd tap the door tenderly to begin with and would soon start banging and pounding until Noori, usually in bed and still sleeping, would croak, "Come in, moron."

But instead it was her sister. Zaheera was a lot like Munazzah: she had the same infectious laugh, the same kind of humour, and the same knowing eyes.

After knocking a second time, Zaheera stormed into the room.

"I know you're awake; you showered two hours ago," Zaheera said, pulling the cover off to examine her older sister in her box spring bed, where she had spent the last sixty minutes staring at the ceiling and wondering about snakes, patronizing fathers, and stupid boys who run from girls.

"You need to get up," Zaheera announced, tilting her head to the side as if viewing Noori from a different angle would get her sister to move.

Noori had no intention of leaving her bed. After what had happened yesterday, between her father and her, and between Noori's and Aamir's lips, she didn't want to face the world. Not until tomorrow night, when she was due to catch her flight. Her dad could try all he wanted; she would still leave.

Everybody in the house knew something was going on, but Noori didn't want to talk about it and, surprisingly, Dad hadn't told anyone about Aamir the impostor, the fake cousin who never existed.

After their argument, they had both sat in the conservatory in silence, knowing that if one of them were to speak they'd start quarrelling again. Dad had placed his warm hand on Noori's shoulder the way he'd done when they had all found out about Munazzah's death. Noori had almost interpreted this small gesture to be a peace offering, but then he slid his palm off and broke the silence.

"Who is Aamir?" he'd asked again. "And what was he doing in our house, sleeping in our bed, eating our food and pretending to be Mai's relative?"

Noori hadn't said a word. She stood up, dragged herself to her room, and that was where she had stayed, skipping breakfast, lunch and dinner. When her mother tiptoed into the room, Noori pretended to be ill, which, in hindsight, was not a good idea. Mum checked her vitals and found nothing wrong with her.

"It's my uterus," Noori had snapped, at which point her mother had left her alone, telling her to get some rest.

Noori was surprised Mum hadn't mentioned Aamir. She was sure Dad would have told her, exposing Noori and her lie. She had found a trace of Aamir in the guest bedroom after he deserted her. A framed picture of his mum as a young woman, the same eyes staring at Noori. The similarities between mother and son were unmistakable. Noori had felt a deep pang of sadness when she had first looked at that photo – how much it must have meant to Aamir. It was one of the few things he had left of his mother. She knew he would miss this. Part of Noori had hoped Aamir would come back, if not to see her, then to pick up the photograph. She had waited in vain.

Apparently Noori was now doomed forever to associate her first kiss with being dumped. Despite it all, she hoped Aamir was OK and would find his way home.

It was not like she could do anything for him now. Her new life was right around the corner. Lahore. Her aunties, uncles, cousins, the new school, lots of novel experiences waiting for her. The timing could not be better; she was more than ready to shed any ballast and move on, pretending this life in Bristol had nothing to do with her. The sooner she was out of here, the better.

"What's going on between you and Dad? We all heard you argue yesterday," Zaheera said, interrupting Noori's internal thought process.

Noori grunted. "Ask him."

"I did and he told me to ask you."

"*Pff.*"

"Is it about the headscarf?"

"I don't want to talk about it."

"Fine." Zaheera nodded, just like Munazzah. "You still need to move, though."

"I'm going to lie in bed all day and eat popcorn with Doughnut."

Noori glanced at the beagle, this loyal creature. He had stayed by Noori's side, knowing she needed comfort.

"We're going to the zoo," Zaheera informed her, turning her back on Noori to amble towards the streaky window that could do with a clean. "One last time before it closes for good."

"I don't want to go to the zoo; I hate the zoo."

"That's why Dad said you have to come."

Zaheera shrugged her small shoulders. Her sister had the same build as Munazzah. They were both petite, unlike Noori, who had always felt like a tree stump in comparison.

"Please come to the zoo; it's our last chance to do something together before you go away," Zaheera said, still not turning round. "The zoo's no fun without you. Mum's at work and I don't want to listen to Hameer and Dad all day. You should hear what they were talking about just now."

"What?"

"I don't know. I stopped listening; it was that boring."

Noori watched her sister, who made no attempt to face her. She felt a weird weight on her chest. The truth was, Noori had neglected Zaheera for months. She'd been a rubbish older sister and hadn't once tried to speak to Zaheera about Munazzah, although she knew she was grieving too. This was her chance to show her sister she cared, possibly her last chance before leaving her and everyone else behind.

Of course, Noori regretted her decision when, half an hour later, she was stuck in the car with her family, the radio playing some crappy song.

"Oh. My. GOD!" Noori yelled from the back seat. "Can someone change the channel or switch off the radio; this song is full of sh—"

"It's full of sh-sh-sh-sh, huh?" Hameer said, sniggering from the passenger seat.

He turned his head and lowered his sunglasses, thinking he was the coolest thirteen-year-old on the planet. Noori knew why Dad, who hadn't said a word to her, wanted her to join them on this family trip. It was his way of punishing her.

Well, perhaps she deserved to be punished. This whole Aamir thing had been a huge mistake. Noori just needed to go to Pakistan now, to feel Munazzah's presence, to say goodbye and hello at the same time. Maybe this was what Rumi had meant by "coming together" when he talked about the moon and the sun. While the two couldn't be with each other, they coexisted in a vast orbit, in perfect harmony, far away from each other but still together somehow.

That stupid song was still playing. Hameer turned down the volume and fumbled around with the radio buttons, glancing at Noori. She knew he was going to piss her off some more. No wonder Zaheera wanted her to tag along.

"Would you prefer some classical music, *Mahnoor*?" Hameer

asked as the sound of an orchestra, accompanied by a set of weeping strings, boomed through the car.

She rolled her eyes.

"This must be Symphony no. 9, 'From the New World', am I right, Dad?" Hameer said smugly.

"That's correct, kiddo."

"Show-off," Noori muttered.

She was the only one in the family who didn't play an instrument and it showed. Her knowledge of classical music was limited. Very limited. Noori was into desi music, real music, not this old stuff that some old dead man had composed hundreds if not thousands of years ago.

Like the music now coming from her handbag. Punjabi, high-pitched, dhol drums, fast beats – Noori's ringtone. She fished her mobile out of her pocket and checked the display. Mai. She hadn't spoken to her friend since she'd left for France. And after yesterday's flurry of texts from Mai, which Noori had ignored because they were all about the alleged distant cousin, Noori wasn't sure whether she was in the mood to talk. Mai would be fuming, and no doubt Noori would have to answer millions of questions about Aamir.

"Answer your phone, will you?" Zaheera grumbled. "And check your messages – it's been beeping for ages."

At that moment, Dad pulled into the car park. It was busy, with lots of hatchbacks and family vans crammed together, but they were lucky and found a free slot close to the entrance. The mobile was still ringing when Dad switched off the engine, and Zaheera was still glaring.

"Bonjour," Noori said, sighing into her mobile.

"You!"

"Hold on, let me find a quiet spot."

Zaheera gave Noori a weird look and threw Hameer a suspicious glance in the rear-view mirror. Even Dad perked up his ears. They were all so bloody nosy. Noori skipped out of the car, gripping the phone and listening to Mai's incessant mixture of French and English. Mai only did that when she was truly vexed.

"You *ne m'écoutes pas!*"

"Say that again?"

Noori mooched off, far away from the twins and her father, who were pretending not to pay any attention to her.

"Do you know what kind of questions my mother asked me yesterday?" Mai shouted angrily down the phone. "Your dad told her about a *relation* of ours who was staying at your house. I mean, *c'est quoi ce bordel!*"

"No need to use vulgar language," Noori said.

"I had to lie to Maman; it was the only way to calm her down."

"I'm sorry."

"What were you *thinking*?"

"I don't know," Noori said. "Things took a turn for the worse after you left."

"What do you mean?"

"I kissed Aamir and saw him naked."

Deadly silence, followed by a rustle and wild rummaging. Mai must have dropped the phone down the side of a sofa, or into the loo.

"I'm gone two days," Mai finally said. "Two days."

"I only kissed him once, maybe twice, and saw him in his, uh, manly glory in your bath."

"How?" Silence. "What." More silence. "Are you out of your freakin' mind?"

"I think it's this whole phenylethylamine thing."

"What?"

"Never mind. Aamir's gone and I'll never see him again. And I am truly and deeply sorry for landing you in trouble with your parents. I'm the stupid friend and you're the brilliant friend." Noori felt a sharp pain in her heart. Mai was the only friend who got her eighty per cent of the time. She'd never be Munazzah, but then nobody could replace Munazzah. Noori had to stop comparing people with her dead cousin; it wasn't fair. "I really am sorry, Mai," she said.

Noori's apology was met with more silence.

"You've almost ruined my holiday. My mum's still mad at me."

"You can blame it all on me."

"I did, moron," Mai said, and hung up.

Noori smiled a weak smile. Things were bad, but they weren't that bad. Mai wouldn't have called Noori a moron if she really hated her.

She shoved her mobile back into her backpack – Munazzah's backpack – and shuffled along, her gaze skipping to the end of the street. Someone was sitting on the orange bench next to a bus stop. Noori squinted, shielding her eyes from the sun. She wasn't wearing glasses today and couldn't make out the figure in the distance, but something about it was familiar.

"Noori!"

Zaheera was flailing her hands about, standing near the entrance and holding up a batch of tickets. Dad and Hameer were nowhere in sight. Noori trotted off to join her sister. When she took a final glance over her shoulder, she couldn't make out the person on the bench any more. A bus had pulled into the bay, and the figure was gone.

46
aamir

This was the third bus that had stopped because the driver thought Aamir wanted to get on. He shook his head at the dark-haired driver who reminded him of Pa and the vehicle took off, Aamir breathing in its diesel fumes. He'd shuffled back up the hill from the harbourside area and was now resting his legs for a moment.

It had been worse hanging around doing nothing, just staring at the familiar block of flats that surrounded Bilal's home. He couldn't stand still. He was wasting nothing but time and his life. Something had to change. Part of him even missed the little bedroom back in Cardiff that he used to share with Bilal – if only he could travel back in time and be a child again.

Maybe his brother had seen his note by now. He would check again soon, and if there was still no key under the doormat, then, well... Aamir could not afford to think two steps ahead. He could barely think one step ahead without getting dizzy. He really was feeling very ill now; sticky in the head and spitty in the mouth, that was the only valid way he could describe his current state. He took a sip of water to soothe his angry tonsils. What was he doing here, at this bus stop, right by the zoo?

The fever played tricks on him, bringing back images and painful memories. All he had to do was look at something and it would remind him of faraway places or people.

Take that thorny bramble bush over there. August was the best time to munch blackberries and these plump ones seemed perfect. Aamir could stuff his face with berries until he burst. Fat, squidgy and dark like a bruise, blackberries were a perfect snack. He imagined popping one in his mouth, feeling each fleshy knobble explode on his tongue.

The moment he thought this, his eyes welled up like a spring. He remembered the last time he had savoured that zesty taste, about a year ago, when he'd meandered through a park in Cardiff with Maa. She always picked blackberries in the summer, carrying a plastic bag in her little black handbag, and a pair of gloves to avoid staining her fingers.

He missed Maa so much. And Mahnoor was right: he'd always miss her. Five years, two decades, a lifetime could pass, and nothing would eradicate the pain. What would Maa make of him now? He'd deserted his family, abandoned everything she'd been a part of and built over the years. The life she had left behind in her native India so her children would have the kind of future she'd yearned for. Aamir had options and opportunities that Maa would have dreamed of when she was his age. And he'd taken it all for granted, never appreciating what he'd had.

The August sun sizzled in the sky, frying Aamir's brain. He had been so stupid. If he could go back to the day when he'd walked out on his father, who'd fallen asleep in front of the telly on his own, Aamir would have made a different choice. He would have stayed. Despite the hurtful words his dad had hurled at him, despite everything that had gone wrong between them, well before Maa's death – Aamir would have stuck it out.

"It's never too late," Mahnoor had told him.

He had to make his way back to Bilal's, but first he had to savour those blackberries and taste his memories before they tumbled into oblivion.

47
noori

"I know you kissed Aamir," Zaheera said, licking the ice cream off her spoon. "I heard you talking to yourself in the bathroom this morning."

Noori swallowed hard. Damn her for always talking too much, even when there was no one to talk to.

"Was it a good kiss?" her sister asked slyly.

"No."

"Oh. Sorry."

It wasn't a good kiss. It was an amazing kiss.

The sisters, who didn't look like sisters, lolled about outside the lemur enclosure, admiring the cute animals. They had lost the others on purpose. After Dad had bought them all an ice cream, Noori and Zaheera had bolted, passing through the monkey jungle until they reached their destination, the lemur walkthrough. Lemurs were Noori's favourite animals, next to meerkats.

"This one looks like King Julien," Noori said, pointing at a lemur who was ogling her vanilla ice cream.

Noori knew her sister would see right through her, but she wasn't in the mood to discuss Aamir. Anyway, there was something else Zaheera wanted to share with her big sister; Noori had felt it all along. The furtive looks she'd thrown her in the car, the way she raised both perfectly shaped eyebrows to get her attention.

Zaheera was studying Noori the way Munazzah used to. As much as Noori had loved her cousin, there had been one thing about her that had unnerved her: Munazzah's ability to watch Noori like a telly. She had always known what channel Noori was on, had always sensed what she was thinking, and right now, as she scraped the last bit of Cornish ice cream out of the tub, Noori was overcome by the feeling her sister had inherited that same eerie quality.

"So," Zaheera said, making friendly eye contact with King Julien and not her sister. "You never told me Aamir was from Cardiff, and not from Edinburgh. Should have realized. He doesn't have a Scottish accent, does he?"

Noori's eyes widened and she tried to conceal her surprise by coughing. She felt a tickle in her throat. Maybe Aamir had passed on his germs during their intimate encounter.

"And you never told me his family was looking for him. Apparently he ran away from home – did you know?" Zaheera asked.

"He was forced out," Noori said. "How do you know all this?"

"Bilal called," Zaheera said.

"Who?"

"You kiss a guy and don't know anything about his family? What would our grandmother say about that? You know her motto. Never kiss a boy until you've met his family, all a hundred of them."

"If it was up to Nani, we'd only kiss one person in our lifetime. Our future husband."

"Yeah, and if it was up to Nani, she'd find us that husband: a good boy from a good doctor family."

Noori suppressed a smile. "You're being unfair," she said. "She'd also accept lawyers or engineers. And self-made millionaires."

Noori loved her nani; that woman was a phenomenon. Mum always said Noori was like her, which wasn't true. Nani was a different kind of animal and belonged to a species of her own.

Zaheera glanced over her shoulder at Dad and Hameer approaching around the corner, both licking their ice creams.

"Anyway," Zaheera said. "Bilal called this morning. Our number showed up on his missed call log and he thought it might be Aamir. He's worried."

Noori shrugged. "Well, that's not my problem."

"You sound like you don't care."

"I don't."

Of course Noori cared.

There was a name for this type of feeling. Rumi used it all the time.

48
aamir

Once, many years ago, he had climbed to the top of the Eiffel Tower and it hadn't ended well. He had puked into Maa's handbag, which was made of brown snakeskin.

Snakeskin.

How ironic.

He didn't remember that detail until he came to a halt at an intersection somewhere in the park. Where was he supposed to go from here, left or right or back the way he'd come? Aamir's sense of direction was usually spot on, but clearly his inner compass was malfunctioning.

He'd devoured those blackberries, even the unripe ones, and now his stomach was protesting with cramps. His entire body felt on fire and the piercing pain in his chest was getting worse and worse.

Aamir staggered onwards.

The sun. So hot. The wind. So cold.

Aamir had never felt this weird before. He wasn't one to get ill; he'd never even missed a class, unless he decided to bunk off school, which was something that happened at frequent intervals after Maa was bitten by the snake.

The snake.

The dog.

The girl with the bright smile.

Maa helping the girl.

Aamir didn't know why he was thinking of the dead girl now as he stumbled along, all alone, on this path that would take him somewhere or nowhere or anywhere. He was delirious; his vision wasn't working; his brain was in a zombie state, half eaten, half alive.

It was almost like he was back in Pakistan, the smoky smell of a bonfire lingering in the air, his feet stamping on the sandy track, whirling up the dust from the rich soil. There was a barking dog coming his way, shuffling along without the owner in sight. Was he dreaming, hallucinating; was the dog even real?

Doughnut.

It looked like the old beagle. Maybe Mahnoor was near; maybe she'd materialize in front of his tired eyes any moment now. Aamir stopped, hit by a sudden wave of vertigo. He was light-headed, feeling like the ground was rocking under his feet.

The dog, it *was* Doughnut. He licked Aamir's dry knuckles, tugging at his trouser leg, trying to get him to move, to guide him.

Aamir took a step forward, stumbled, and felt his weight shift.

He couldn't stop the fall; it was too late. He was losing his balance and he had to protect his head; rugby had taught him to always shield his head. People died every day of a fall. And Aamir was still falling, feeling the grubby soil under his elbows, landing against something hard. A rock.

A wall of darkness engulfed him.

49
noori

All at once, Noori found herself on her own with her father while the twins disappeared to go to the loo. The last thing she wanted to do was spend time with her dad. She was already dreading tomorrow's two-hour journey to Heathrow. They hadn't really spoken to each other since yesterday.

"Your mother and I had a talk last night," he said, finally.

She glared at him. "About what?"

He lowered his knobbly chin to get a better look at his daughter, who was amazed she was capable of having a conversation with her father without feeling the need to scream.

"Your trip to Lahore," he said, sniffing. "She knows I have my concerns and I still don't want you to go. However, if you absolutely must leave, I don't want to stand in your way."

Noori couldn't believe her ears. How had he changed his mind overnight? Her mum must have given him a proper talking-to. She would have loved to know what she'd told him – that he needed to let her fly and not clip her wings? Noori was almost lost for words. On the one hand, this didn't change anything. She would have gone to Lahore with or without his approval. On the other hand, it showed Noori that her father might have thought about his daughter's words. He wouldn't stand in her way, he had said. If this wasn't news… Did it mean she'd forgive him? Well, that was a different matter.

"The other thing we talked about was your friend Aamir," Dad said.

"He's not my friend."

"So who is he?"

"He's just a guy whose mother died, all right? And his father chucked him out of the house so he doesn't have a proper home. He likes Rumi and cricket and he makes incredible rotis and he's a bit of a coward, but ultimately he's an OK person."

Dad stared at her as if she had just recited an oath of allegiance, pledging her loyalty to the monarch. Noori was sure she would have been interrogated further if her father's mobile hadn't started ringing. He was still frowning at her when he answered the phone.

Within seconds Noori knew something was wrong.

50
aamir

Something was wrong. Aamir was semi-conscious, or so he thought.

He could feel someone touching his shoulder, saying, "Mate, you all right, mate?"

He could hear barking – Doughnut, whose damp snout was nudging him in the side.

He could taste oily blood in his mouth.

And he could feel his heart giving up the ghost.

Aamir tried to open his eyes, fighting against the growing darkness.

Something was wrong, very wrong.

51
noori

"Doughnut," Dad said, in the piercing voice he employed when in panic mode. "Haqiq just called."

"Uncle Haqiq?"

Noori thought of the kind old man with his beagle. The last time he had telephoned to offer his condolences, after Munazzah died. Whatever had prompted him to call now had to be serious. They were still near the monkey jungle, the four of them. Zaheera and Hameer had come back and were just watching their father in confused silence.

"Haqiq," Dad said again, wiping a film of sweat from his ridged forehead. "He just went out for a walk and found Doughnut tottering along the pavement. He's escaped; the dog's escaped!"

"Maybe it wasn't Doughnut," Zaheera said reasonably. "It could have been a different beagle."

"He knows Munazzah's dog. He tried to stop him, but

Doughnut ran off," Dad said.

"No, that can't be right. Doughnut's at home. It's nap time and he never misses nap time," Hameer said.

"He can open doors; we all know that." Noori looked at Zaheera. "You were the last one to leave the house – did you lock up properly behind you?"

"I…" Zaheera scratched her temple, her face riddled with guilt. "I'm not sure."

Noori had a bad feeling. What if a car ran Doughnut over? What if he got lost and never found his way home again? Doughnut was such a silly dog, but he was the only dog Noori had ever loved.

"We have to go look for him!" Noori said, panicking. If Mai found out what had happened, especially after the Aamir incident, their friendship would be officially over. And Munazzah? She'd die with worry if she weren't dead already.

The Oates clan all knew what it felt like to lose a family member, and Doughnut had become an instant part of their tribe when Munazzah first brought him home from an animal rescue centre. He was their responsibility.

After they scurried to the car in a frenzy and drove back home, Dad breaking various traffic rules, they all split up. Hameer headed west, Noori went south, Dad veered north and Zaheera took a right turn, facing the east of town, roving around the leafy streets in search of Doughnut. They must have looked like a bunch of desperate oddities, stopping random passers-by and asking them whether they had seen a doughnut.

Why had the silly dog bolted out of the door on his own,

and was he looking for them like they were looking for him? Doughnut was a bit senile, or so Noori believed. Why else would he pull at the leash every time she took him for a walk, guiding her to Munazzah's former home in the hope she'd still be there? He needed help. She had to find him.

Noori was jogging around the Downs like a maniac, moisture dripping down the back of her neck, the headscarf soaking up beads of sweat. She had checked all of Doughnut's favourite places. The ancient oak tree he always weed against. The filthy bin he liked to sniff, excited about the gross smells he was able to detect. A tiny mousehole he poked his nose into every single time he spotted it.

She was close to giving up. The only hope that remained was Doughnut finding his way back on his own. He still possessed enough brain cells, right?

"Noori! Stop!"

Dad.

Noori saw her father's bulky figure approach. Their paths crossed in the middle of the grass. No Doughnut. So he hadn't been successful either. The members of their search party had agreed to ring one another if they tracked him down and Noori kept checking her phone, hoping she'd get a call.

Dad wheezed up to Noori, his face pink as a plum. He didn't look happy and she tried to put their differences aside now they were both preoccupied with Doughnut's welfare. Dad's shirt was showing sweat marks in the weirdest spots – near his bulgy navel area and around his moobs. He was huffing like he'd run a marathon, bloated cheeks and all.

"Can't." Pause. "Find." Another laboured pause. "Doughnut."

"The twins might have more luck," Noori said, feeling a tiny bit sorry for her elderly father. At forty-six, he had probably lived half of his life and it showed. His condition was deteriorating with each year. His hair was thinning, his waist was expanding, and his brain had crashed.

"I." Pause. "Need to sit."

Dad plopped onto the ground. Noori was looking for an ice cream van so she could buy him a lolly to get his energy levels back up, but no luck. She could only make out a wailing ambulance in the distance.

"We've lost him," Dad said, wiping something from his eye. "Doughnut's gone. Munazzah's dog."

"Are you crying?" Noori said, towering over her father. Deep down, she wanted to give him a hug. "Get a grip. Doughnut will be all right; it'll all be all right in the end."

He glanced up, his eyes filled with hope and the odd tear. "You think so?"

I've no idea, she thought helplessly.

"Of course," Noori lied. "Doughnut's smart in his own dumb way. And he wears a dog collar, so someone will find him and return him, I'm sure of it."

Noori wasn't sure of anything. She was so confused and anxious, she could hardly remember her own name, address or hair colour. And Dad wasn't helping. He was quietly weeping now. The last time she had seen him cry, which was also the first time she had seen him cry, was when they had found out about Munazzah. He had hugged all three of his children then, no doubt counting his blessings that his kids weren't dead.

"Man," Noori said, handing him a tissue from her backpack and a cinnamon-flavoured piece of gum. "There's no need to freak out yet."

He blew his nose, nodding his head and stuffing the strip of chewing gum into his mouth.

"I'm so sorry," he said.

"What for?"

"Everything." He sniffed.

This wasn't about Doughnut any more.

"I didn't mean what I said about you being unstable." He added another sniff, casting a wistful glance at his oldest child. "I'm scared to lose you, Noori, scared to be away from you. My job is to look after you, that's all I care about. And it hurts me so much to see you hurting. I just want to make things better for you, and how can I do that when you're thousands of miles away?"

Noori felt a lump in her throat. Her dad could be so dramatic, but the truth was, he had never spoken so candidly to her before. She almost wanted to slap him on the back for being so open, although deep down it made her uncomfortable to realize her father needed her more than she needed him.

She was a fledgling now, ready to leave her nest. And her dad was the equivalent of a mother hen – fussy and interfering when he only meant well. A Rumi verse came to her then, visiting her like a fleeting memory. "I grow silent. Dear soul, you speak."

He looked at her then, she looked at him and they both communicated in silence that they would *try* to forgive each other. Noori knew her father had regrets, and she had regrets too. She didn't fully understand him and he had never understood her. But, for now, they had to move on; bigger things were at stake. Maybe once they had found Doughnut, they could talk and not shout at each other.

Dad reached out a hand and she helped him up. This was awkward, their weird moment of reconciliation. She was glad when her phone started ringing.

Hameer. There was a crackle of background noise on the line.

"Have you found him?" Noori asked.

Noori heard a bark. Doughnut! She'd recognize that silly yelp anywhere.

"I have," Hameer said. Why did he not sound relieved?

"Is Doughnut OK? Is he hurt? Does he—"

"There's nothing wrong with Doughnut," Hameer cut in, suddenly using his grown-up voice. "It's Aamir who's not doing well."

"Aamir?" Noori asked, confused.

"He's here. Doughnut found him, or he found Doughnut, and then I found them both and—"

"What's going on, Hameer?" Her voice trembled.

"The paramedics are here," he said. He started stuttering, as if he was in shock. "Aamir is unconscious. There's a lot of blood. I think he's hit his head."

Noori felt like she'd swallowed a ball of air and tried to

push it out of her lungs. Breathing was not easy. Thinking was not easy. Aamir. She knew he'd been sick when she saw him last, but had he been *that* bad? And no wonder Aamir was unconscious if blood was involved – he had almost fainted over a drop of blood when she first bumped into him.

"Where are you?" Noori asked, trying to think straight.

"Ladies Mile," Hameer said.

Noori glanced to her left. Ladies Mile was a long stretch of a road, but Noori was near by. She squinted into the distance, spotting an ambulance. Blinking lights. White and yellow van. That had to be them.

"We're coming," Noori said and hung up. She signalled at her father, muttered the words "Doughnut" and "Aamir" and then darted across the dry grass, feeling the bristly blades brush against her ankles. She was gripping the phone, digging her nails into it, listening to the beat of her heart, the sound of her feet thumping on the ground. Her headscarf fluttered in the wind, threatening to fly away.

She had almost reached the ambulance and could make out her brother, hands in his pockets, head hanging low. A nervous Doughnut was by his side, tail stuck between his legs, barking at the paramedics, who were carrying a person on a stretcher.

Then Noori saw him. Aamir: motionless, his long black hair sticking to his neck and covering half of his face, his cheeks drained of colour, stained with soil and dark crusts of blood.

DAY 7

52
noori

Noori was dying. She couldn't detect her heartbeat and her physiological senses were faulty. She had lost the ability to feel, touch or smell, which meant her nervous system was shutting down. That's what happens right before death kicks in, and the last sense to go is the ability to hear.

Mum had told her this. After Munazzah died, Noori had wanted to know whether her cousin had felt anything, whether dying hurt. Of course it bloody hurt. Noori was infested with pain, except her body tried to protect her from the agony by numbing her other senses.

Aamir.

He was causing Noori's internal death. The moment she'd seen his limp body on the stretcher … and now he was lying in the intensive care unit. There was something wrong with Aamir's heart and brain. Yes, he was ill before, but there was also some kind of heart condition that had gone undetected, so Mum had said. And then he had fallen, hitting a rock at a particularly unfortunate angle, leaving him in a critical condition. In a coma in fact. They had to perform an operation and didn't know when he'd wake up. *If* he'd wake up.

If she hadn't seen what was going on, she would have found the whole situation quite difficult to believe. Ridiculous even. Just like Munazzah and the snake bite, and that was definitely real. Aamir ending up in Mum's hospital out of the blue – this was the kind of plot twist she'd relish in a Bollywood film, but not in real life where this kind of preposterous drama was rare.

It didn't look good. Mum had told her so.

Noori knew what her mother meant by *not good*.

Aamir was a trauma patient now.

And his Glasgow Coma Scale was worrying, especially his pupil reactivity score.

That was what Mum had whispered to Dad last night when she thought Noori was out of earshot. Acute subdural haemorrhage was the term Mum used to describe Aamir's current state, a rapid form of bleeding causing pressure to rise within the brain – which can result in loss of consciousness, paralysis or death. That kind of thing is common among old people, and young adults are rarely affected, unless they're involved in a serious accident.

"Poor Aamir," were Mum's words.

Her parents didn't care any more whether Aamir was Mai's distant relative or not. They had liked him, Mum said, although they had wished Noori had been honest with them from the beginning. Parents have to say those things. But for once Noori was grateful they had left it at that. It was Dad who had called Aamir's brother, Bilal, to let him know what had happened. And Noori was grateful for that too.

"Is Aamir going to die?" Noori had asked Mum this morning over breakfast.

"Darling," Mum had said. She paused. "Aamir's in good hands. The doctors are keeping a close eye on him."

"You haven't answered my question."

At that point Mum had pulled Noori in for a hug. She had wanted to stroke her daughter's hair, but ended up stroking her headscarf instead. Mum had said something unexpected then, as she studied Noori. She told her a little story – maybe to distract Noori, maybe to pass the time, maybe to impart a nugget of wisdom.

"I used to wear a headscarf when I was your age," Mum had said, still holding Noori in a tight embrace. Noori's nose was pressed against her mother's neck and she sniffed her skin, absorbing that lovely oriental rose fragrance that was Mum's signature scent. "I thought a good Pakistani girl should wear a headscarf, you know, but then I realized I wasn't a good girl and I'd be better off being a good person – and being myself."

"I never knew you wore a headscarf," Noori mumbled.

"That's exactly what Munazzah said when I told her."

"Why do you think she suddenly decided to wear one?" Noori asked. "She never explained."

"You know what she told me?" Mum was smiling now. "I'm not making this up – you know what your cousin was like. She said to me, '*Phuppo*, the real reason I'm wearing a headscarf is to protect my crown chakra.' And then she started giggling. I don't know if she was serious, our Munazzah; she was a funny girl."

Noori remembered her mother's words now as she was making her way to the hospital to see Aamir. Was Noori a good person? Did her crown chakra need protecting from evil forces? She scratched her head/headscarf. Maybe she'd know one day, but not now, when she was in Dad's Volvo en route to the hospital, desperately worrying about Aamir's health. Doughnut was lying in Noori's lap. He whined, placing a firm paw on Noori's hand as if to comfort her.

"We're almost there," Dad said, breaking the sombre stillness at last; clutching the steering wheel tightly, he had been lost in his own thoughts like everyone else. He had insisted on driving Noori, and the twins had decided to tag along. They liked Aamir, Zaheera said. He was a cool guy, according to them, and a Mister Kapoor lookalike.

But being with them all, in this metal box of a car, felt claustrophobic. The minute her father rolled into a parking space, Noori flung the door open and jumped out without uttering a single sentence. She had to see Aamir on her own.

"We'll wait in the cafe!" Dad shouted after her.

They were all supposed to meet Mum there, but Noori wasn't going to hang around. It was not like she had time on her hands. The plane. Her new life. Lahore. She had to be at the airport in eight hours, giving her just enough time to say goodbye to Aamir. She wanted to see him one last time.

She swooped through the hospital doors and the pungent

smell hit her in the face like a twenty-tonne bus. She could never get used to that odour, that blend of prayer and love, of curing and hurting, of living and not living. It was sweet and sticky and damp. It was like dug-up soil, earthy and raw.

Noori knew where to find the intensive care unit and she knew Aamir's room number because Mum had told her, but she didn't know what to expect. Visiting hours were flexible, but the number of people allowed in a patient's room wasn't. And Aamir's father and brother would be there.

Noori wasn't keen to barge in on Aamir's family. They wouldn't want her there; she was a stranger. Noori didn't plan on staying long anyway. The longer she was by his side, the harder it would be to leave. She just wanted to know how he was doing, what he looked like, whether he'd wake up if she touched his hand or whispered in his ear.

Noori approached the door and pressed her cheek against it, unable to make out any sounds. Her fingers trembled as she pulled down the handle and peeped into the room. The smell was worse in here, more daunting, like swimming into the current of a brisk sea. She slunk into the room, her shoes tapping the ocean floor, her body swept along by the undertow, the water rushing in and out of her ears.

No one was with Aamir. Was this person with the swollen face and a bandage wrapped around his head really him? She would have to inch closer, be brave and look past the feeding tubes, the IV lines, the drains and the monitoring equipment. He was breathing in a funny way, looking so pale, like a ghost. And where was his long hair? They must have chopped it all off.

The bruises, the cuts on his hands, the chipped fingernails: Aamir wasn't wearing his armour now. His shell had been shattered, and all that was left was this breathing mass. The air was clotted with sad regret. No, Noori couldn't stay long. She had to get out before her knees collapsed under her and she sank into the ground, the ocean swallowing her up, burying her alive.

Just one touch, one last moment of contact. His arm, so floppy and weak. She would have to be gentle. She stroked his hand, feeling the soft ridges of his knuckles, tracing the lines on his skin, the criss-cross pattern, the fabric that had been woven into his soul.

Three letters, tattooed on the bottom of his thumb. Noori had never noticed them before: *i o u*. What did that mean? Did Aamir owe someone, or vice versa? Did he think he owed Claire, his pa, his maa? She'd probably never know now; perhaps this was just another grain of sand that would lie forgotten on the dead seabed.

"Who are you?" a male voice boomed behind her.

Noori spun her head round, unable to see, her vision blurred, the salt water stinging her eyes. Her sight improved as she blinked away the tears, and she stared at the two frowning men gripping cups of coffee who were scrutinizing her.

One man looked like Aamir's older doppelgänger and the other looked like Aamir's older, older doppelgänger. They had to be father and son. Bilal, and his dad.

"Are you Noori?" the younger man asked.

She nodded.

"Your mum, we just met her; she said you were going to visit," Bilal said. "You're Aamir's friend?"

Noori nodded again.

"Without your family we wouldn't be here now," Bilal went on. "We wouldn't—"

And at that precise moment, an alarm went off. A machine that was attached to Aamir started beeping and before she knew it, Noori and the two men were ushered swiftly out of the room as a team of medics rushed in, yelling instructions at one another.

Aamir.

Lost.

In the ocean.

53
aamir

Was he a goner, swimming around in a dark ocean? He kept hearing voices.

This was not what he'd expected. The last thing Aamir remembered was seeing Doughnut's wrinkled face and falling backwards onto something hard, a spiky stone or a sharp rock. He must have knocked his head badly, but it hadn't hurt. When Aamir thought about it, he realized he must have lost consciousness quickly. And now he was trapped in here, whatever *here* was.

He couldn't detect his hands, mouth or feet because his body had disappeared.

How strange it felt to be lifeless but still be alive. For years he had believed in nothing, and now here he was, floating around in space, wedged between light and darkness, caught in a weird twilight zone. Part of him, a tiny baby part, hoped he'd see Maa again. If there was such a thing as an afterlife, she would have picked him up right by the golden gate. But she wasn't here.

Damn, he must have ended up in al-A'raf, that place between paradise and hell, some kind of purgatory. He should have taken his religious studies more seriously when he was alive, should have listened to his father, who had tried to make him believe in things Aamir never put his faith in. But then it wasn't the teachings that taught people the truth; it was the experience of truth that taught the truth.

And then, of course, there was Mahnoor. He'd never see her again, and what was the advantage of being dead when you couldn't spy on the people you cared about? He would have sent Mahnoor messages. A flower, a feather, a lucky ladybird perching on her windowsill.

That was when Aamir realized for the first time that he was in love.

And he wanted to be.

Those voices, they were getting noisier, conveying a sense of urgency. He tried to listen, but how could he hear without ears?

Aamir knew he couldn't stay in this twilight zone forever. Something was dragging him away from here. Night would fall, and darkness would cloak him soon. That voice: he knew it. It would have brought tears to his eyes, if he had been in possession of any visual organs.

"Aamir."

Someone was calling him, and Aamir followed.

54
noori

"Aamir," Noori said, gazing up at Bilal and his father. "How is Aamir?"

The two men stared at her and she felt a heavy weight in her chest, trying to break free. At least she could sense her heart again. It was pumping the way it was supposed to, unlike Aamir's. His heart rate had dipped, which was why the alarm had started beeping and all those medics had stormed into the room.

And now Noori was here, standing outside the intensive care unit, pacing around a brightly lit corridor, blinded by hospital lights. Bilal and his father looked like kind people. Sad people. Devastated people. Why had Aamir run from them? Why had he run from her?

"How is Aamir?" the father muttered to himself. "He is in the hands of God, the Almighty. Allah will save my Aamir, inshallah."

Bilal placed a hand on his father's shoulder, comforting him if only for the moment. The sadness, the weight, the fear, all this was reflected in this small gesture. Bilal had given up on Aamir, was preparing himself for the worst. Noori saw it in the way he pitied his father, who wouldn't stop clinging to hope.

She tried to read the silence between Bilal and his father, but she only heard white noise. Something about the situation she found herself in was other-worldly. She felt a strong sense that she had been guided, that she was supposed to be here somehow, standing beside Aamir's family in the hospital.

"It is God's will," the father said, nodding at this son, the one who wasn't dying.

"Mr Mahmood?"

A nurse appeared behind Aamir's brother and father, holding a file close to her chest. She squinted at Noori, giving her the same sympathetic glance she had offered Bilal and his dad, no doubt believing she was family and belonged here, with them.

"My son," the father said, his voice cracking. "How is he?"

"He…" The nurse hesitated, now switching her attention to Bilal. "I'm sorry, but Aamir…"

The hospital transformed into a massive black hole, swallowing up light and darkness.

All was quiet.

The last sense to go before death kicks in is the ability to hear.

And Noori heard no more. She ran from the deafening silence.

55
aamir

Aamir would send her a sign.

Mahnoor needed a sign.

They all needed a sign.

56
noori

The headscarf had to come off; there was no point donning it now. Noori felt like an impostor wearing it; she didn't have the right to drape a scarf over her mane, especially when she had lost all her faith. The universe had screwed her up, along with her crown chakra.

Why had Noori ever believed that by adopting a headscarf she'd find her true way and become who she was supposed to become? Noori was still the same Noori, except she had lost her heart and she didn't know if she'd ever get it back. Those words – the ones the nurse had uttered – they echoed through her head, reverberating louder each time she tried to shut them out.

And now Noori was here, all alone in the hospital car park, feeling like something had been ripped from her insides. Staring at the ground waiting for it to swallow her up, until she noticed that thing by her feet – what was that?

She stooped over a delicate flower growing out of a crack

in the asphalt. It was blue; it was beautiful; it was a bluebell. A bluebell in August? Impossible. That arched perennial with its cluster of blooms blossomed in April and May, not late summer. Her mum had taught her that. Her fingers pinched the stem and, with a gentle tug, she drew the little wonder towards her. It was a miracle, wasn't it?

Meeting Aamir had been a miracle.

The fact she had run into him on Munazzah's bench as if she was meant to meet him; as if she was meant to have her broken heart broken again. And where should a heartbroken Noori go from here? Lahore, of course. Anarkali's tomb, that symbol of broken hearts. She scanned the busy car park, spotting her father's dark Volvo. She had to find her family.

Noori shuffled to the main entrance with slow, steady steps. The sun danced high in the sky, daylight reflecting off the large windows. Noori narrowed her damp eyes, peering through the glass at the group of people in the cafe who were directing their attention back towards her. Dad. Mum. Zaheera, Hameer.

And then Bilal emerged behind the sad quartet. She lumbered inside.

"We were looking for you," Dad said, taking a hesitant step towards her.

Noori heard her father's concern, but she couldn't feel it; she was numb. The twins were analysing her, the way they always did, drawing conclusions based on their interpretation of the leafy data-tree. And Mum did her doctor thing, assessing the patient with care, without dumping her own sorrow on Noori.

Bilal was the only one who didn't stare at Noori with pity.

His grief was greater than hers. He had known Aamir forever, and Noori could claim no more than seven days, *seven days* that had changed everything.

"Noori, *meri jaan*," Mum said, her voice soft and tender. "You've met Bilal, haven't you?"

Noori nodded.

"Do you mind going with him?"

"Going where?"

"I know this sounds strange," Bilal said, all calm except his tongue was out of tune. "But my father would like to speak with you."

"Talk? Now?" Noori was stuttering.

"It won't take long." Bilal mustered a smile, albeit the saddest one Noori had ever seen. "He's with Aamir."

57
aamir

There was this Rumi poem that came to Aamir's mind. He didn't know why he remembered it now, but it was the only thing he could think of, the words spinning in his head.

> Never lose hope, my heart, miracles dwell in
> the invisible. If the whole world turns against
> you, keep your eyes on the Friend.

And Aamir kept his eyes on the Friend.
Mahnoor, his soul friend.

58
noori

"Does … your father want to know whether Aamir told me anything?" Noori asked. "Whether Aamir blamed him?"

Bilal nodded. He looked so defeated and sad, and Noori couldn't stand it. She couldn't stand being around herself. She heaved out a heavy sigh. What was she supposed to do but oblige a father who had lost a son?

"Could you ask your dad to come out?" Noori said, staring at the door behind which she pictured a lifeless Aamir. "I can't go in there again, not with Aamir…"

Bilal tipped his head to the side, swallowing. "What do you mean?" he asked.

"Aamir's body, I don't want to see it."

Bilal frowned. "Aamir's body? You know… He isn't dead."

Noori stared at Bilal, unable to comprehend his words. Of course Aamir was dead. She had heard the nurse saying something about Aamir's heart rate dipping, using a term that sounded like cardiac arrest. Hadn't she?

Aamir.

"The doctors," Bilal muttered, "they said we should pray for a miracle."

"Miracles are not uncommon; they happen every day, everywhere, all the time. Look here," Noori said, holding up the bluebell.

Bilal peered at the flower, giving Noori a questioning stare. Sure, he didn't see the significance of a flower blossoming at the wrong time of year, but Noori did. A miracle wasn't that difficult a feat. Aamir's heart was still beating, and that alone was a miraculous thing.

"I think we should go in," she said.

Bilal nodded. He probably thought she was a nutcase, but she didn't care. Miracle workers didn't occupy themselves with trivialities. Noori had bigger things to focus on now. A timid knock on the door, and she tiptoed into the room.

Aamir's dad twisted his head round, staring at Noori. Bloodshot eyes, sticky hair, grey stubble on his chin – the ultimate look of a man who loved his son more than anything else in the world.

"Abbu," Bilal said, addressing his dad in a low voice. "Do you want me to get you another cup of tea? You look tired."

"I'm fine, *beta*," he said. He spoke to Noori. "Come in." He waved his hand, beckoning Noori further into the sterile room.

Noori stepped in, followed by Bilal. They both slouched into the uncomfortable plastic chairs, their heads turned towards Aamir, who had never looked so much at peace. Was it selfish to want him to hold on? Who knew what state Aamir would be in, should he open his eyes.

"Thank you for coming," Aamir's father said. "I've not been able to introduce myself. I'm Malik Mahmood."

Noori nodded.

"And Aamir – you're his friend; you saw him before the accident?"

"Yes," Noori said, and paused. She considered addressing him as Uncle – that's what Munazzah would have done, but Noori wasn't Munazzah.

"Do you know what happened to him, before all this happened?"

"He…" Noori didn't know what to say. "Aamir said he had to leave home for a bit."

Malik Mahmood glanced at Bilal, whose face was streaked with pain. His eyes drifted to his younger son. Noori was sure Aamir's cheeks had had more colour in them when she first entered the room. And with each second, he lost more of the paint that tinted his skin.

"Did Aamir say anything about us?" Malik Mahmood asked. "We argued; I—" His voice cracked.

What could Noori say to make them feel better? She didn't want them to think Aamir had abandoned them out of hate.

"Aamir felt ashamed," Noori said. "He felt guilty, but he wanted to go back home and work things out. That's why he called Bilal."

Noori detected a hint of relief in both their expressions,

but it was of the bittersweet sort. What good did it do to hear this detail now? Maybe one day it would ease the guilt she could feel in the air, but not today.

"Let us say a prayer for Aamir Inayat Mahmood," Aamir's dad said, bowing his head.

It was the first time Noori had heard his full name. Never would she let it go.

Bilal and his father closed their eyes, lowering their chins and moving their lips though no sound escaped. They were deep in prayer, leaving Noori to stare at Aamir.

She was searching for subtle clues. A tear, a smile, all she needed was a twitch of his fingers, a clear sign Aamir could feel them, despite being trapped in his palsied body.

Noori tried desperately to come up with positive thoughts, so she could mail these happy thoughts to a still Aamir. He didn't look like he was slumbering. It wasn't like the time she had run into him napping on the bench. Back then he had looked sweet and scruffy. Now all Noori could see was his vulnerability.

Did she imagine the faint glow surrounding him, the soft light engulfing him, keeping him safe? Maybe she'd been staring too long into the fluorescent bulbs and was hallucinating, seeing the dim aura hovering over Aamir. Either way, he looked at peace, and he had never looked at peace when he was awake.

So many facts were still missing. Noori didn't know all of the basics about Aamir, like his age, or goals or wildest dreams. But in a way, it didn't matter. Noori didn't have to know every detail about Aamir because she understood the bigger picture. She saw him, in his entirety.

Noori felt it again, this deep and tender connection to Aamir. Rumi had written about such soulful bonds, and now she understood what the Sufi poet had meant when he wrote about being bewildered by the magnificence of someone's beauty, of being drenched in a flood of longing, of love being the water of life, making the heart a place of prayer.

Plea. Pleas. Please.

Please save Aamir.

Please protect him.

Please return him.

Noori would promise anything if it meant Aamir would be OK. She'd never watch *Anarkali* again, would never argue with her parents, and she'd even give up her dream of becoming a playwright. Hell, if he opened his eyes, she'd not even get on that plane to Lahore. Whatever would be asked of her, Noori would comply.

She knew she was bargaining, haggling with a force so much greater than life. Negotiating with that force was a stage of grief, and Noori was familiar with grieving.

What would Rumi say?

The old turbaned poet mumbled into her ear, a silent murmur echoing through her blurry mind. "Never lose hope," a kind Rumi whispered, winking at Noori and lightening her heart, "miracles dwell in the invisible."

Pause. Rewind.

Miracles dwell in the invisible.

Do you hear me, Aamir?

59
aamir

The light flashed. It was time to depart.

Miracles dwell in the invisible.

1 YEAR LATER

the tomb

Smoggy Lahore, Pakistan: the most chaotic and picturesque city Noori had ever laid eyes on.

She was loitering outside Nadira's, aka Anarkali's, sumptuous tomb, which her lover, the Mughal emperor Salim, aka Jahangir, was said to have built for his one true love.

Noori still fancied tragic love legends – the sadder, the better. A real love story wasn't complete unless one of the lovers died. As much as she craved fairy-tale endings, Noori knew that not everyone was granted a happy ever after.

And the whitewashed tomb, magnificent as it was, memorialized love and its inevitable heartbreaks. The building was a masterpiece of Mughal architecture, circular in shape, adorned by semi-octagonal towers and roofed by a noble dome. It had once been surrounded by a luscious garden, and Noori felt a warm floral note of pomegranate blossom drift past her.

Anarkali was the Urdu word for pomegranate bud. Noori must have imagined that seductive scent flitting past her nose because there weren't any pomegranate trees in sight, just some nondescript shrubs and palms, and a couple of potted plants.

Noori didn't know if she wanted to enter the building that was now used as the Punjab Archives Museum, after once accommodating a Sikh ruler and being converted to a church during the colonial rule of the Raj. She had mixed feelings. For years she had yearned to visit Anarkali's tomb, where facts and folklore melded to create a love story as beautiful as it was heartbreaking.

Maybe Noori didn't have to enter the mausoleum. Maybe it was enough to observe the place from the outside and imagine the inside. Historians contested Anarkali and the prince's love story. They said it never happened, or at least not to this extent. And they claimed the cenotaph inside the tomb was not at all the final resting place of Anarkali, housing perhaps the remains of one of Jahangir's wives. Who knew and who cared? No matter what modern scholars declared to be true, Noori didn't doubt for one second that there was passion and love between those two lovers who were never destined to be together. Circumstances, people and rules kept them apart. But despite this, Anarkali and her prince would always be in each other's hearts.

"Ah! could I behold the face of my beloved once more, I would give thanks unto my God until the day of resurrection," the prince was said to have inscribed on the marble sarcophagus.

And wasn't this a token of real love; didn't it speak of his heartache of losing his one true lover?

Ah! No! I shall not step into Anarkali's tomb, giving thanks unto the prince for making me weep in public, a misty-eyed Noori thought, wiping a single tear from her cheek. These days, she wasn't in control of her tear ducts, feeling overcome with wild sentiments out of the blue.

Her trip to Pakistan had been an emotional one, and she had saved Anarkali's tomb for last. Noori had visited Munazzah's burial place in Lahore first, finding a white downy feather next to her grave. She took it as a sign, because Noori believed in signs. They guided her when she was in need of guidance. She also spotted a black snake, slithering into a hole next to a muddy river. Was that a sign of something too?

Snakes, ancient symbols of rebirth and transformation, were considered to be guardians in some cultures, offering protection. And their poison was used as medicine, turned into an elixir to aid healing, holding the dual power that could both cure and kill.

She'd work it out one day, the meaning of it all, but now her time in Lahore was drawing to an end. Noori would board a plane to Heathrow tomorrow, where her parents and the twins would be waiting for her. And she would tell them about the happy memories she had made here, in Pakistan.

Noori had stayed with her auntie enjoying hearty meals and late evenings with her, sipping pink Kashmiri tea, lounging on her rooftop terrace and listening to the hums of a bustling city that never slept. She had met jovial relatives she hadn't known existed and Noori promised them she would come back. Soon.

Lahore, this busy city built on ancient lands, had attached itself to her heart. The music, the smells, the sights, the flavours, the people. It wasn't just the rich architecture, the lively bazaars, the gorgeous gardens, the roadside eateries, the beautiful shrines and mosques, the blend of Sikh, Hindu and Muslim heritage that had left a surprising mark on Noori. It was the earth, the water, the heart and the soul of this place that had buried itself deep into Noori's DNA.

One half of Noori belonged here, and one half didn't.

The half that didn't belong would start university in a few weeks. Noori had enrolled in a programme back in Bristol, studying drama writing because she still loved drama; it was in her blood. The part that did belong here would haunt her at night, coming to her in dreams, filling her with nostalgic desire.

A gentle breeze fluttered past, lifting Noori's pink veil. She had last worn this particular headscarf on *that* day. About one year ago, on a hot August day, in a hot hospital room in Bristol, when Noori had prayed for a miracle.

"When I said you should wait for me, I thought you'd wait for me!"

Mai. She was stomping towards Noori, dressed in a traditional salwar kameez, and it suited her. What didn't suit her was the headscarf. She had tied it into a knot and placed it on top of her head. It looked ridiculous.

Mai was Mai.

And how could she have gone on this trip without her friend? But Noori wasn't going to lie. Spending three weeks 24/7 with Mai had taken a toll on her sanity.

"Why didn't you wait?" Mai asked, stabbing a finger into Noori's side.

"You were taking forever," Noori said. "How many selfies did you shoot – two thousand?"

"Tais-toi!"

"You don't have to tell me to shut up just because I'm right."

Mai sniffed. She was grumpy because she was missing Doughnut. Noori missed him too.

"Why are you looking like that?" Mai asked, her tone less hostile.

"Like what?"

"Like you were just thinking of him."

"Thinking of who?"

"You know who."

Of course Noori had been thinking of him. How could she not think of Aamir? She was in Lahore, standing under the hot sun, gazing at Anarkali's tomb, remembering Nadira and her Jahangir, those two lovers who had starred in the greatest and saddest love story of all time. It was only natural for her thoughts to stray to Aamir.

He was her first love, and always would be.

Noori's mobile was ringing, that familiar Punjabi song trilling across the grounds of Anarkali's tomb. It would be Auntie Shaima, checking up on her. Noori and Mai weren't supposed to venture far on their own. Auntie would be anxious, but there was nothing to be concerned about. Noori felt safe here. She was with Anarkali and the prince, and their love lingered, in the invisible, bringing bliss to people who were open to receive such wondrous blessings.

"Answer your phone!" Mai snapped. "You don't want your auntie to freak out; she's so sweet, and old, and I don't want her to worry, all right?"

Noori rolled her eyes and answered her mobile, bracing herself for what was to come.

"Hey, Auntie."

There was no reply, but someone was breathing heavily into the phone.

"We're still at Anarkali's tomb, but will be back for lunch," she said in Urdu.

Again, no reply, just another sniff.

"Auntie, are you OK?"

"So how's Anarkali and her lover?" the voice asked, in English. "I bet you've been bawling your eyes out, thinking about their stupid love story."

Noori grinned. "No."

"Don't lie to me."

Noori was still grinning, wiping away that one single tear.

"I can't wait to see you tomorrow," Aamir said.

"And I," Noori said, "can't wait to see you either."

Noori's eyes wandered to Anarkali's tomb, the ultimate symbol of tragic love. The best love stories, she had to admit, were the ones that ended with a miracle.

Acknowledgements

Seven Days is the product of many things. I was guided by love and grief and hope when I wrote this novel, cheesy as it may sound. So many people impacted my writing. Fellow writers. Unsuspecting strangers I fleetingly passed in the streets of Brussels or Paris. Dead poets (cue: Rumi!). Loved ones, including the spirits of those who have passed.

While it's impossible to thank and acknowledge everyone, there certainly is a list of people I would like to emphasize my gratitude to, and since I haven't won an Oscar, I'll keep this short.

First, I want to say thank you to those who have made *Seven Days* a reality: my stellar agent, Davinia Andrew-Lynch, who championed this book from the start and gave me countless pep talks when I needed them most. To the wonderful team at Walker Books: a huge thank you for believing in Noori and Aamir's story, with special thanks to Frances Taffinder, Emily McDonnell and Annalie Grainger.

I wouldn't be writing this without the support and love of family and friends from various parts of the world: thanks for allowing me to talk your ears off about the random dilemmas of a writer — Christine and Yasmin, I'm looking at you!

My siblings — Shabnam, Shahjahan, Zishan and Jahanghir (plus their significant others, Maja and Selina) — danke für euer offenes Ohr! I am also eternally grateful to my parents, Rocchina and Islam, who always encourage their children to reach for the stars. Thank you from the bottom of my heart for your unwavering love and faith in me.

As I'm nearing the end of this shout-out, I would like to thank my husband, Jerrauld, who patiently listens (at least I think he does), offers sound advice (at least I think he does) and cheers me on, no matter what.

And last but by no means least, a heartfelt thank you goes out to my most treasured daughters, Carys and Malia. It is your light that lights my world.

Photo by Lorena Schaupp

Rebeka Shaid was raised in a multicultural household, surrounded by piles of books, nosy siblings and lots of mythical trees that are known as the Black Forest. Growing up she wanted to be a snake charmer or ventriloquist, but that (luckily) didn't pan out. Instead, she turned to words and writing. After doing sensible adult things like going to university, working as a business journalist and becoming a mum, she decided to pen a YA novel. In her writing, she likes to explore themes of identity, loss and coming of age. Rebeka lives in Germany. Visit her website at www.rebekashaid.com